GW01071735

Soul of a Butterfly

A NOVEL

SAFAA BAIG

Soul of a Butterfly

A NOVEL

BY SAFAA BAIG

TRIM TABBERS

Published by Trim Tabbers Publications

ISBN: 978-0-9927991-0-6

For every butterfly out there,

those who have been and those who will be,

and those who are;

enlivening the world with a flurry of colours each day.

May you fly, flutter, and soar.

May Allah grant you the
best in this life & the next!

love,

[signature]

Acknowledgments

If there is one thing I know for certain, writing this novel as a teenager was unquestionably, undeniably, and beyond a shadow of doubt impossible to accomplish without the consistent and limitless guidance from Allah every step of the way, followed by the never-ending support I received from my family and friends. This book would not be in your hands if it were not for them.

All Praise and Gratitude is to Allah, the Most Magnificent, the Most Merciful, the Lord of Majesty and Bounty; the One and Only Creator. The One who guided my pen, inspired my thoughts, and answered my every supplication. Du'aa was the ink to my pen and without it, this book would not be in your hands. Indeed, Allah Alone is Sufficient for us, and He is the Best Disposer of affairs (for us).

I am forever indebted to my parents: Aamir Usman Baig and Farah Naz Saghir, for supporting my writing, for believing in me steadfastly and for of course bearing with me and my 'writer' mood swings. To the coolest grandfather in the world, Qaid Saghir [aka Nana], you may not be here anymore but you were and always will be my first mentor and best friend, and my forever inspiration. To my late grandfather, Usman Baig, and my beautiful grandmothers, Na'eema Baig and Rehana Begum, for every wisdom and advice showered upon me.

To the coolest [and wackiest] siblings in the world – Yusra; for all those truly animated late night stories and perfectly enacted retellings of novel plots, I can never stop listening to you, Abdullah; for just being my big brother, you shall inspire many cool [and annoying] 'brother' characters for years to come, Hiba; for happily playing partner to all my crazy ideas and stories, for lending me a listening ear and company to laugh with, you are and always will be my number one reader, Azzam; for cracking jokes a mile a second and making me insanely laugh, yes, you're *awesome*, and finally Aasiyah; for just being the littlest and for making my world more sparkly each and every day. Love you all heaps and heaps.

Sincere thanks to my phenomenal English teachers - my dedicated mother to begin with; for always encouraging my imagination to run free and my pen to scribble it down, Naheed Amir; for making English my favourite subject as a child and opening my eyes to a world of wonder and possibilities, Hajierah Issack; for igniting within me a newfound love and respect for poetry and literature, and Baiyinnah Sideeq (Umm Zakiyyah) for constantly motivating and encouraging, inspiring and mentoring me into the writer I am, going way beyond the call and duty of an ordinary English teacher, and becoming more than just a teacher, but also a friend, a sister, and a role model.

Huge mega-ginormous thanks to my dear friends – Maariyah Baig, Amina Hussein, Meryem Demirkaya, Hirra Gilani, Rumsha Usmani, Amani Basha, Rida Salman, Hajra Nadeem, Amel Fatine, Qudsia Mall, Rasheda Dreyton, Sumbul Rafiq, Madiyah Rana, Hannan Hassan, Shaaista Mahomed, and the entire team at YMP; thank you for just being your awesome selves and I truly feel blessed to have you all in my life.

JazakumAllahu Khairan [because thank you just does not equate] to each and every one of you for everything.

And finally, last but definitely not least, I owe my utmost gratitude to those who made du'aa for me. That is what kept me going, and at the end of the day, it is only that which really counted most.

"I only ask to be free. The butterflies are free."

~ Charles Dickens

Chapter One

"Katieeeee! Wake uuup! Come down quick. I've made waffles, and you know how fast they finish!" I heard my mum call out.

Waffles? Did she just say waffles? I'm dreaming, I thought, as I sluggishly yanked my eyes open, and checked the time. Nine in the morning, oh yes, definitely a dream.

"Katieeeeeeee! Maaaark! If you don't come down right this minute—"

"O-kaaay! I'm up! I'm up!" I yelled back, as I rubbed my eyes sleepily and crawled into the bathroom. Glancing at myself in the mirror through half-lidded eyes, I sighed, I really need to get some sleep. Just then, the smell of freshly baked cinnamon rolls wafted into the bathroom, and my eyes sprang open. Swiftly, I yanked my long blonde hair into a high ponytail before rushing through my daily cleansing routine, and hurried downstairs.

Yawning noisily, I stumbled into the kitchen to find my work-a-holic mum whipping up a jug of banana milkshake. Wide-eyed, I froze for a moment, staring at the kitchen scene before me as if transfixed, rubbed my eyes again, and then blinked twice for good measure. "Uhh....mum. What's with the food? Something special today?" I asked, gazing around at the waffles, pancakes, freshly squeezed orange juice, and delicious-looking cinnamon rolls on the breakfast table. My mum turned to face me and beamed, "No. Nothing special, just your average healthy breakfast at home. Why? Don't you like it?" she asked, biting her lips.

"Yeah, sure, but normally our 'average healthy breakfast at home' is a bowl of Frosties and a Coke," I said slowly, wondering what on earth was wrong with my normally 'self-assured, make-your-own-breakfast and you-are-what-you-eat-so-here's-a-coke' mother.

"Well...I..." my mum started, quickly forming a juicy lie in her mind but then just as quickly changing her mind as she glanced at my narrowed eyes. "I read this article in the newspaper that said fifteen percent of teenagers these days leave home because of the awful breakfast. And I'm not saying you're *leaving* home or anything, because you wouldn't have any reason to, but just so that you feel more comfortable with your *home* so that there really will be no reason for leaving, because I mean you wouldn't....you're not an average teenager...," she rambled on as fast as she could.

"Yeah, I'm far from average. Do you have to rub it in my face?" I teased, reaching around her to grab a glass.

"Oh, honey...I was joking. Of course you're not err... different, you're an average teenager who would never have any idea of leaving this house, right?" she circled her arms around my shoulders and smiled so widely that it hurt to know she couldn't hide a secret. Oh yeah, she was definitely up to something.

"Oh, dearest, I would never ever have any idea of running

2

away; I mean my god this breakfast just looks *absolutely, unutterably ,indescribably* mouth-watering. You wouldn't mind if I stayed here for the next ten years, would you?" I asked, putting on a serious face, before turning around to cover my laughter, and taking a big gulp of milkshake.

"Katie, of course I'd love that and you'd be more than welcome—" she stated, laying a hand on my shoulder, "Wait, what are you…are you *laughing*?" Whipping me around to face her, she narrowed her eyes angrily.

"You don't have to make fun of me! I'm just trying to be a good mum. You're practically anorexic and you should eat more!" she scolded me.

So that's what all this was for, because I'm…wait…did she say *anorexic*?

"What'd she do now?" asked my annoying older brother, Mark, as he walked into the kitchen in his usual morning disarray.

"*AAAnorexic!!!* What do you mean anorexic? Can't you see all this fat?!" I spat out indignantly, pulling at my stomach which unfortunately seemed to have shrunk in the last few minutes.

"You are!" she shot right back.

Mark looked at us strangely, "Okay…*mum* she's definitely anorexic but you didn't have to say it to her face and *Kay*…," he took one look at my furious face and simply said, "Chill, would you?"

That was the final straw. "Chill? *Chill?* You chill!" I lunged at him.

My mum pulled me back, "Katie, he doesn't mean it! Really, Katie, let *go*!" she cried. It was sort of fun, like a 'tug of war' game. Mark tried to pull away from my iron grasp and my mum tried to pull me away from yanking his hair out.

"*Mum,* he called me anorexic!" I yelled, completely forgetting that she had too.

"Mark, go to your room," she said.

"Wha...wha...you said –" he started, but was interrupted with a "Go now!"

"What about breakfast?" he asked so dejectedly that she managed to smile slightly.

"Ummm...fine! Sit down and eat! But don't you dare say a word!" she exclaimed, and then turned her attention back to me.

"Katie, you want to eat now?" she asked hopefully.

"You just want me to eat 'cos you think I'm anorexic," I replied back snottily.

"Honey, I'm sorry. It's just that you're really not eating these days, and I know that as soon as school restarts after the half-term holidays, with all the recreational activities and going to friends' houses, not to mention those crazy outdoor trips your Dad takes you on, you'll get even thinner. I'm sorry, everything I said was rubbish. Forget I said anything. I mean look at you, you look even bigger than me," she cooed at me. I beamed and was just about to ask "Really?" when Mark snorted. That did it!

I went over to the glossy black kitchen table and smacked his head into his plate of waffles. Silence. My mum gasped and then started to giggle, which started me off. He picked his head up and glared at me as blueberry syrup slowly dripped down his face. I smiled angelically and sat down opposite him. "Serves *you* right."

He got up. "You are dead meat!"

"You wanna fight, huh?" I stood up into a karate position and held my arms in front of me as defence. He just stared at me.

"Huh? You scared, Mark Anderson? You think I can't karate chop you right this minute. You're wrong. Yeah man, I got moves you never seen before. I'm real good. Dad taught me," I said, hopping from side to side. Honestly, I only knew a few punches and hand twists and was beginning to wonder how long it would take to run back upstairs. What if he really did take up my offer? I looked up at Mark then, sizing him up. Oh boy, when did he get so big? Suddenly, his face creased with laughter as he pointed at me, and he continued to hoot for a full two minutes, every once in a while, looking at my bewildered face and starting off again. Annoyed, I went up to him and threw a few punches. Nothing. My mum joined in on the laughing, leaning on the spotless white kitchen counter.

I rolled my eyes as my mouth twitched slightly.

"Ah, I'm seeing something," Mark grinned knowingly at me, "Wait, is that a smile?"

"Shut up," I laughed, shoving him aside as I sat back down at the table.

He went off to wash his face, still laughing, and my mum sighed, "To think it took me a whole hour to make this breakfast and now it's cold and ruined."

I smiled at her sweetly. "Don't worry. As soon as sparky comes back here, I'll give him a few whacks and he'll gobble it all down."

"Just try me," Mark said, a grin still on his face, as he returned to his chair.

"Nah, I don't want to damage that small brain of yours and stop you from getting into university which would mean *away* from me, or hurt your face which sadly already resembles Frankenstein's. I do wonder sometimes," I smiled mockingly, "how can we possibly be related?"

"*This* small brain happened to get all A's in his exams and Frankenstein's got a special date in half an hour. So there!"

"No way! *Liar*," I replied, eyes bulging out, shaking my head. Honestly, I was gobsmacked; I mean, not that Mark isn't good-looking and all, but it's just that he's been described as something of a 'heart-breaker' in the past year, which makes these dates quite rare, to say the least.

Mum says that me and Mark used to look like a pair of chicken legs, skinny, scrawny kids with thin straw-coloured hair dangling off our heads, small noses and tiny eyes, but then one summer we 'blossomed' and when we went back to school we were suddenly noticed not just for our looks but for everything else that we're special for. To me, it just sounds like a 'You're-the-most-special-kid-in-the- world' lecture that mothers often give, though my mum likes adding in a few gruesome effects to make it sound more real. Dad, on the other hand, says we've always been good-looking and normally winks at me when he says it, also adding in a "You know who you got that from, huh Katie?" Parents, you never can figure them out. Having divorced when I was six, I'd always take turns asking them the same questions, 'How do you know the Earth is round? Why don't animals speak? Who invented school? Where is God?', and believe me, getting completely different answers from them left me pretty troubled.

So now, a smug Mark, at six feet two inches, smirked down at me from his side of the table. Somehow over the years he'd had a tremendous growth spurt; in addition to this, his thin straw-coloured hair has been replaced by soft ash blonde hair slightly skimming his shoulders. His playful spring green eyes, which he inherited from my mother, were now sparkling with triumph as they dared me to question him further, needless to say he has many a times been described by my classmates as a 'hunk'. I narrowed my deep sky blue eyes at him and threw my straight golden hair over my shoulder, reminding him that only last week I'd been invited out on four dates, and refused all of them on account of not being in the mood. I lifted my heart-shaped face high in the air and stuck my tongue out at him. If he had inherited my mum's beautiful features, then I had definitely inherited my dad's. Most people say I'm his mirror-image, not just in looks but in personality as well.

Gulping down another glass of banana milkshake, I quickly turned to the remaining cinnamon roll on my plate, finished it off, and then pushed back my chair.

"Well, I'm off. It's a Fridayyy!" I sang, plonking my dish into the sink and giving my mum a quick peck on the cheek. "Thanks for the spectacular breakfast," I said, before trotting up the stairs to my room. Pulling on a pair of Levis quickly, I flung open my wardrobe and scrimmaged around until I found the black t-shirt from Topshop that I was looking for. Dashing in front of the mirror, I let loose my hair and shook it about, then finished off my look with some Rimmel lip gloss and Maxfactor eyeliner. I glanced at myself in the long six-foot mirror my dad had bought me a year ago and smiled, not bad.

Not bad at all.

"Hello, Ellie. Would you be a dear and help me out?" I heard a scratchy voice coming from my right, just as I shut the front door.

I turned to see who it was and found myself smiling at Mrs Willow. She's an ancient neighbour of ours and knew my mum, Eleanor, when she was little, hence the 'Ellie'. She often says I resemble my mother so much that I remind her of her, the fact that I quite clearly look like my dad though has brought me to the conclusion that she doesn't want to bother learning a new name, or that she doesn't like him. On the plus side, hearing her call Mark 'Arthur' always sends me into a fit of laughter.

"Yes, of course. How can I help?" I grinned at her, as I walked up to the wooden fence that divided the two houses.

"Winnie's gone!" she gasped, grasping my hand tightly.

Winnie is her cat and drives Mark bonkers. Whenever Winnie goes missing, which is ninety per cent of the time, she begs Mark to go look for him. I remember the last time it happened and

Mark ended up going down four blocks searching for her and when he finally came home, he'd screamed, flopping onto the couch, grass sticking out of his hair, as he glared into my laughing face, "Old Mrs Willow lost that wretched cat again! I searched every corner, street and park within a mile's radius. And where did I find her? Huh, Katie?"

I'd meekly replied, "In the back garden."

"Y…yes. How'd you know?" His anger instantly dissipated as he stared at me in confusion.

"Because he's been there every other time you've gone searching for him, stupid," I'd laughed.

Now as I looked at Mrs Willow pointedly, I asked, "Have you checked the back garden?"

"Of course! Now don't you go on like Arthur, I checked it twice," she nodded her head proudly. I smiled politely as I stood there waiting for her to let me search Winnie's favourite hiding place.

"All right, go on in. But I'll tell you now, I doubt—" she started but I'd already rushed into the garden in search of Winnie. My eyes searched around the massive back garden in which Mrs Willow had made sure to plant every type of flower known on the planet. I jogged up to the small rosebush on the left side and smiled, "Ah, Winnie. Come on out."

I ran back up to Mrs Willow, handing her the cat as she stared dazedly at me, still finishing her sentence "—you'll be able to find him there," and then hurriedly sprinted out of the house and onto the neighbourhood street.

"I'm going up to Kings Mall, see you later!"

I ran up to the nearest bus stop and fell on the bench, trying to catch my breath.

"Katie?"

Hoping with all my heart that Mrs Willow hadn't followed me, I looked up to see a squinting Christy behind the wheel of a bright orange Aston martin. Her platinum blonde hair had been woven into a complex French braid and her crystal emerald eyes hidden beneath a pair of large Mont Blanc sunglasses. Christy Milano is a classmate of mine and easily one of the most popular girls in our school. I've known her since nursery school and we've never really gotten along, to say the least. While she play-acted 'Queen Christy' during classroom breaks, showering her admirers with expensive gifts, I ran around playing 'tag' and leading the rest of the classroom on wild adventure games. So now, even though we both rank about the same level of popularity, she's constantly competing for 'Queen bee' status. What we do not rank however is the same lifestyle, the spacious four bedroom house I live in located in Belgravia is nothing compared to her stunning seven bedroom mansion in Mayfair, complete with a pool, cinema and boasting a good ten thousand square foot, and happens to be just one of houses. And that is exactly why I was not looking forward to her seeing me, sitting at the bus stop, on a Friday morning.

"Christy! What are you doing here?" I yelped, my voice sounding an octave higher than usual, as my mind scrambled around for some excuse to feed her.

"Oh, just came to drop off some charity things at some organization Daddy's funding," she said, disgustedly.

10

"Charity?" I asked, surprised.

"Oh yes…Daddy said I had to. I don't know why he even wants to give them clothes. I mean, it's not our fault they're poor, and personally, I think handing out designer clothes to them isn't going to make them anymore richer or anything," she grumbled, a mixture of hate and irritation in her voice.

I raised my eyebrows slightly.

"Don't look at me like that, I'm serious. So what are you doing?" she asked curiously.

"Oh...well…," I coughed, realizing quickly that I was completely out of ideas, "I…umm…I was just going up to…to… Kings Mall," I mumbled.

"Kings Mall?" she wrinkled her nose, "Why would you want to go *there*?"

Now, Kings Mall is your ordinary Mall, with ordinary shops, and ordinary people. But you see, Christy had never really considered herself ordinary, and so the idea of one of her 'friends' going there was quite…blasphemous.

"I….umm…need to pick up some groceries," I improvised on the spot, "...from errm…Sainsbury's!"

"Oh." She smiled politely, as if realizing then just how vastly different our lives were, "I see."

I smiled back at her tightly and then turned my head in pretence of looking around, hoping with all hopes that she'd leave now.

11

"So, how are you getting there?" she asked.

I looked at her dumbfounded and then at the bus stop where I was sitting and then back at her.

Her eyes widened in astonishment as she put the pieces together, "A *bus*. Oh god! Katie, are you sure you want to be seen in that? Come on, I'll give you a ride. You never know about public transport nowadays. So dangerous," she shook her head at me pitifully, moving aside a pile of magazines that were taking up most of the seat next to her, and then beckoned me over once more.

I stared longingly at the polished car and let out a sigh. "That's sweet of you, but I can't."

"Oh yes, you can. Hurry up," she exclaimed. I shot her a gracious smile, just as her eyes began to glance fleetingly around at the people nearby. I followed her gaze and quickly realized that people had begun to stare. It wasn't every day that a girl in an Aston Martin picked you up from the bus stop.

"Katie, I said come on!" she repeated for the third time, making it sound more like a demand than a request. In that moment, it dawned upon me that what I'd considered to be Christy's generosity was in fact her desire to keep up appearances. Still, I was not someone who gave up a free ride in an Aston Martin.

"Umm...sure thing!" I replied, forcing a smile and settling myself into the seat next to her.

As she drove, we gossiped about teachers, classmates and 'normal' girls.

At last, we reached the Mall, and I thanked her once again for the ride. I strolled inside, her cursory gaze following me, and then spent the next five minutes in Sainsbury's purchasing bubble gum and a pack of crisps for myself, just in case she happened to follow me inside. Finally, after a quick peek outside to make sure she'd left for good, I turned and made my way to Primark - home to some of the coolest fashion clothes at a cheap budget. Life sure isn't fair.

Chapter Two

"Mo-om, I'm home!" I yelled loudly as I stumbled into the house carrying a load of groceries in my arms, a week later.

"Yes, yes of course, I understand. Yeah, she just came back so I'll tell her now. No, she's busy putting away the groceries, so she'll call you later. Okay now. Bye." My mum sighed as she put the phone back on its cradle.

"Your dad can be such a pain sometimes," she mumbled as she got up to help me.

"Was that him on the phone? And Sam told me to tell you they've got an 'All You Can Eat' lunch at Ringo's tomorrow," I said as I swung the fridge door open with my leg, two milk cartons in my hands.

"Really? That's just great. I wanted to stay on a little longer

14

after work and now I don't have to make lunch," she smiled, eyes gleaming.

I laughed. So typical of mum, she'd do anything to be able to get out of cooking.

Mark, who was hurriedly typing on his laptop in the living room, yelled "Can I bring Joe and Tony with me?"

"Yeah sure, my treat!" she yelled back, still grinning.

"So, was that Dad on the phone?" I urged impatiently.

"Oh yeah, I forgot. He said he wants to pick you up tomorrow and spend the weekend with you. But...," her smile slowly crept away as she spoke.

"Great! That's super! I haven't seen him in ages, who knew his six week trip to Morocco would turn into six whole months. Did he say when he's coming over?" I interrupted her excitedly and was mumbling to myself when I remembered the low 'but'. "W...wait you said but? But what?" I asked, anxious now.

"Well, love, he...he said he has to talk to you about a few things and that I should maybe expect you to be back early. You know, you might not like what he has to say," she hesitated as she spoke, watching me carefully for a reaction.

"A few things? Expect me back early? No, he probably just lost the semi-final tickets I gave him a month ago. They're showing soon but...I didn't really want to go and I mainly got them for him," I replied, still excited though burning with curiosity. I wondered what he wanted to talk to me about; he was well aware that I wouldn't really sweat over those tickets.

"Yeah well, don't expect it to be so small. He sounded pretty worried. And…" she was leaning towards me now and started whispering "… Mark's been pretty low since he met your father two days ago."

"Yeah, well whatever. No use sweating about it now, Mum. Oh, by the way, did Jayne call? She had some 'gotta-tell-you-now-or-I'll-die' news for me." I strolled into the living room and picked up the phone.

"Yeah. She's been calling ever since you left. What's that about?"

Jayne Collins is my all-time best friend; we've known each other ever since our exhausted mum's potty trained us, been through thick and thin together (if that's what you call bad hair days and excited tennis tournaments), and are practically like sisters now. I know every item that lies in her bedroom and every lipstick in her makeup drawer and she knows all the channels on my TV and exactly what ticks off Mark.

The phone rang right then, signalling Jayne's growing impatience.

"Hello, who is it?" I sang happily.

"Who do you think?" she replied angrily. "I've been calling you for the past three hours. Where were you?"

"Oh, just went out to get us some groceries and I did a bit of window shopping too. Did you know Topshop's got a new line out? Gorgeous stuff. How about you?" I replied cheerfully, plonking myself down on the living room sofa and grabbing the TV remote from Mark's loose hand.

"Topshop's got a —" she began, side-tracked for a moment and then quickly reverted back to her sour tone. "Are you *trying* to make me mad?"

"Nope." I smiled, dragging the word out.

"Well, do you wanna know or not?" she asked with an edge of indifference, though I knew inside she was itching to tell.

"Well…that depends…," I started.

"Dad bought Jeff the car he wanted!"

"What?!" I screamed, sitting up instantly and causing Mark to jump out of his seat. "Mercedes Benz SL 600?" I asked breathlessly.

"Yes!" she screamed animatedly.

"No! *No way*. Oh my god. You've got to be kidding me!" I yelled.

"And you know what that means…," she squealed as I finished her sentence, "We get to ride in his car."

"Man, this is so great. We don't have to ride in Mark's trash anymore and we get to show it off when school starts! Oh, this is terrific. Congratulate him from me," I said, bouncing with excitement and ignoring Mark's angry scowl.

Jeff is Jayne's older brother *by five minutes*, he's as close to me as Mark is. Sometimes it's hard for Jayne to keep up with us as we rant on together about our favourite movies, books and music. We both cheer for the same football team while Jayne paints my toenails and visit sleek car showrooms while Jayne goes perfume shopping. I'm not saying Jayne and I aren't close, but he's as close as it gets to a second best friend. And believe me, having twins as best friends can be side-splitting sometimes. They have no resemblance whatsoever and are on pretty good terms with one another, aside from the occasional teasing from Jeff. Jayne and I have always been in the same class, which may be one of the reasons we're inseparable, but Jeff has some incredible IQ or something and was immediately put in a higher year when he started school; he also happens to be the captain of our school's football team.

She laughed, "Jeff wants to talk to you. And I've got to check out the 'Zara' sale with mum right now, so I'll talk to you tomorrow. See ya."

"All right, bye." I laughed, shaking my head at her shopping addiction.

"Hello?" I heard Jeff's deep voice on the other end.

"Jeff? Congrats! You're so lucky. I mean, SL 600? That's like... wow. What'd you do to convince your dad? No wait, you got a scholarship right? Oh my god. You're just too lucky. I heard it has a —"

"Whoa. Kay, slow down. You're talking too fast. Start from the start, what were you saying?" he asked, his voice tinged with amusement.

"Yeah so, umm...congrats. Nice car. Good Grades. Can't wait to ride it," I replied back casually, the excitement still in my voice.

"Thanks. You're gonna love it. It's exactly your type," he replied graciously.

"Pfffft. Of course it is. I'm the one who recommended it to you!" I laughed at his ignorance, so typical of boys.

"Yeah, sure you did. As I recall, you wanted me to get the McLaren SLR. Which my dad would never get, seeing as it's double the price," he replied, and I could picture him rolling his eyes at my 'so-called' stupidity.

"Yeah, well whatever. It's still a Mercedes; I guess it's just too bad my taste is more expensive than yours," I huffed, smirking inwardly.

His answering laugh was cheerful, "You got that right, Kay. Don't know where I'd be without your *superior* taste in cars."

"That's right. Don't ever forget." I laughed back, enjoying the moment.

It was always easy talking to Jeff, I loved that I could be myself, not having to explain my actions all the time and that he appreciated me for who I was, as was the same with Jayne.

"So umm... are you staying home tomorrow?" he asked, still chuckling softly.

"Yeah. I mean, why wouldn't I?"

"Oh, I was just wondering."

We were quiet for a few seconds; I was thinking frantically, wondering if there was a huge party I'd forgotten about.

"Yeah so, you with your dad this weekend?" he asked curiously, a hint of impatience in his voice, signalling why he had initially

19

wanted to speak to me.

"Yeah. It's gonna be absolutely great, he has some surprise planned for me. Maybe he's planning a trip to Bristol or Leicester like last time," I gushed happily.

"When are you coming back?"

"I don't know. Next week some time, maybe. Why?"

"No reason."

"You're not telling me something. What happened? Is something wrong?"

"Nah, you're always jumping to conclusions, Kay. Let's just say I've…. got a surprise for you too. Monday morning, 7 o'clock sharp, my place. Be there." He said, matter-of-factly and then hung up.

Two surprises with the weekend closing in. What more could a girl want?

Chapter Three

"Dad! Where have you been? You were supposed to call the minute you got back. You promised," I scolded him over the phone, only seconds after answering it.

He chuckled, "Hey pumpkin, I missed you. I was going to call but…I got caught up with a few things."

"Like?"

"You'll know in due time."

"*What*," I asked with exaggerated annoyance, "is up with all this secrecy? First Mark, then mum and now you —"

"Guess what? I've got a surprise for you."

"You know that's not gonna work, Dad. I'm not a child anymore, so stop —"

"Look outside your window."

"What?"

"I said look outside —"

"Why?" I interrupted him, turning my body so that I was now facing my bedroom window. I peered at it cautiously, wondering if he'd planted some sort of prank there.

"It's a surprise," he sang softly, obviously incredibly amused by the scenario.

"No," I replied, folding my arms defiantly as if he was actually there, watching me.

"All right, well then..." he drew out his words, sounding surprised, "you're missing out. Big time. I mean, who knows what could be lurking behind that window —"

"Dad, I am so not falling for —"

"I mean, do I know? Yeah. But do you? Nah, not so much."

"Dad."

"But then again, that's just the choice you've made. And I've got to respect that, even if it means you're missing out on something irrefutably astounding and unquestionably phenomenal —"

"Oh, come on! Dad, don't pull out the vocabulary card. That's not fair —"

"It saddens me to inform you of this, but Katie, my dear, *you* are a bromide."

I gasped, "I am not!" Mentally, I was wondering if he'd made up that word or if it actually existed. "I am not a *bromide*," I said again with more vehemence, "I am the farthest thing from a *bromide*," I continued, pulling a dictionary out from my bookshelf and flipping through it speedily, "if ever there was a person who was a *bromide*, it would not be me, for I am not a —"

My dad laughed at the other end, "You won't find it in the dictionary."

I scowled, "Fine, well then —" and stopped mid-sentence as I heard a loud honk outside. Furrowing my brow, I opened my mouth again, only to be stopped short again by another honk, this time sounding suspiciously as if it was coming from outside my window. Standing up slowly, I moved curiously towards my window, and pulled back the curtain in one swift move.

"You were saying?" he asked, as I suddenly caught sight of a very familiar red Honda Accord Euro, with my dad seated inside, grinning broadly.

I burst out laughing as I watched him wave at me comically. "Nice surprise, huh, Katie?"

"Best surprise," I giggled, "Give me five minutes and I'll be down."

"No need, I'm coming in. I have to talk to your mum about a few things. Take your time," he replied, stepping out of the car.

"A few things? What?" I asked, impatiently.

"Just need a few words with your mum. Okay, I'm gonna hang up now… because I'm here for goodness sake," he laughed loudly and then hung up.

I smiled to myself and skipped downstairs to welcome him. I reached the bottom of the staircase just as Mark opened the door and my smile slowly crept away as I saw Mark's face turn livid.

"What are you doing here?" I heard Mark demand, and I instantly slowed my steps.

"I came to get Katie… look, Mark, it doesn't have to be this way. It's…I…I miss you," my dad said gently, his cheerless eyes resting upon Mark's.

"This is the only way, Dad…Jack. Katie will be down in a few minutes. You can wait outside," he remarked gloomily, as he began to close the door.

"Wait! Mark, what do you think you're doing?" I asked angrily as I ran up to the front door, pushing Mark out of the way to allow my dad in.

Mark glowered at my dad as he coldly replied, "Don't let him get to you Katie," and stomped out of the room.

"Now, see, that's someone I'd call a bromide," I winked, "Don't let *him* get to *you*, okay?"

He laughed as he pulled me in for a tight hug, "I missed you so much, Kay."

"It was your own fault for staying in Morocco for six months," I joked, my voice muffled against his shirt.

"Architect Extraordinaire on the job," he grinned, holding me back to look at me. "You've grown."

"You say that every time you see me," I rolled my eyes.

"No, I mean it —"

"What's going on? I just saw Mark fuming in the living room," my mum inquired as she suddenly walked into the room, a look of surprise on her face as she noticed my dad.

"Oh, you're here early," she said, seating herself onto the sofa.

"Drama, Drama, Drama. Dad needs to talk to you."

"Yeah, there are a few things I need to discuss with you," he added, then taking in my inquisitive eyes, chuckled, "Privately."

"Oh sure, that's nice. Get rid of me already. I'll be in the living room," I sighed as I went off to question Mark on his strange behaviour.

I entered the room headstrong, a sharp retort on the tip of my tongue, but as I glanced at his face, I immediately held back. If his face hadn't looked so blank and empty, I would have demanded an explanation for the rude encounter he had had with my dad but the expression on his face just wouldn't allow me. There was a mixture of sorrow and regret etched on his face, but knowing him, his stubbornness and determination to 'always be right' would not push him to apologize. His eyes stared at the university applications he intended to fill in but hadn't started, and his hands were clasped tightly as if in pain. I turned my head towards the TV which I noticed now was on, Manchester United was as always in the lead and the Chelsea players seemed too out of the game to play well. I gently sat down and picked up the remote, flipping through the channels, one at a time.

After a few minutes of restless impatience I switched it off and lay my head back, only to suddenly hear my mum's low angry voice, "No Jack, this is wrong. She'll flip. Why'd you have to do this? No wonder, Mark...Yeah? Well, you should have asked them first! How could you do this to them? After all that's happened..."

Her frantic accusations grew louder as the seconds drew by. I held my breath, eager to eavesdrop on something more but only heard my father's low soothing voice and then nothing. I waited and waited, breathing as softly as possible just to hear a bit more, Mark too had lifted his head and was now curiously looking at me, as if to ask what I thought was going on. I shook my head at him in a 'how-should-I-know?' way and sighed, "Why aren't you talking to Dad?"

"None of your business," he replied, his face once more rigid and all the curiosity wiped away.

"It *is* my business. Dad's back after six months and you just blow him off? I have a right to know. So tell me, or I'll just squeeze it out of him." I'd had enough of all the glances my mum had been giving my brother recently, the way Mark wouldn't answer his calls, and now this?

"You do that." He had now gone back to his formal position and avoided my scowling eyes.

"I don't think there is a single brother alive who could be more infuriating than you," I said coldly and then left the room in a huff. Dad would explain everything, he usually did. As I got closer to the room, I noticed that the voices had died down and all was silent. My mum was standing in the kitchen making a cup of tea for herself as my dad shrugged on his coat.

"Oh. I was just coming to get you. Are you ready? We should be leaving now," my dad said, attempting a smile that didn't reach his eyes. I scanned his face, but there was no trace whatsoever of the fact that he had a lot of explaining to do. I didn't know where to start.

"Yeah, I'm ready. Ready to hear what you have to say," I crossed my arms.

"Not now, Katie. I'll tell you in the car," he replied, averting my gaze and suddenly in a hurry to get out of the house.

I threw my hands in the air, "Fine then!" I went up to my mum, whose body was turned and gave her a quick hug. Sensing that something was still wrong, I whispered in her ear, "I'll be back by Monday. You think you can manage without me?"

"Haven't I always? Have a good time, love." She turned around and squeezed me happily, "You can come back whenever you want. Take care of yourself," she held me longer than usual, and I managed to notice her sudden reluctance to let me leave.

I looked at her curiously and then picking up my cream Guess bag, which I had packed earlier on, and turned to leave. My dad was waiting in the car and my mood suddenly shifted back to the situation on hand.

I slid into the car and turned to address my dad. "I want to know everything, don't leave a single thing out. And don't tell me it's none of my business because it is."

He started the car silently, and as we moved forward, he looked out of the window. After a pause he spoke, "This is tougher than I imagined. Are you sure you don't want me to tell you once we're home?"

"Now," I replied with a tone of finality.

"I'm Muslim."

At first, I thought I'd heard wrong and blinked a few times. I smiled slightly, expecting him to laugh at his idea of a joke. He didn't, and so I searched his face, my eyes darting here and there for any sign that he was joking. Not wanting to hear more and not wanting to believe him, I laughed nervously, "Sure, Dad."

"Sweetie, I'm being serious," he sighed, taking a quick look at my teasing smile that had now frozen as thoughts cluttered my mind. "My trip to Morocco didn't just help me with my work; I found a reason to live. At first, I thought the people there had such bizarre, outlandish customs, I mocked their religion. But slowly I realized it was the truth. It became so clear. I never really was a practicing Christian like your grandfather, so all my life unknowingly I'd been searching for something. Something that had *meaning* because my life had none, something real... *the truth*. And Islam... *Islam is the truth*."

I dropped my gaze to my lap, "I don't believe you," I replied back hastily, whilst knowing in my mind that there was a certain level of sincerity I detected in his voice. I shut my eyes tightly as my mind screamed with fear, fear that he might not be joking, and fear that he really was a *Muslim*.

28

"Katie, we all have a place in this world, a reason we were put here. Life isn't random, it has *purpose*. I found mine. Look back two weeks honey, haven't you noticed anything?" he asked softly, brushing my hair back from my clammy forehead.

I wondered carelessly, sifting through my memories for everything that had just happened.

Dad gone.

Six months.

Morocco.

Islam.

Mark upset.

Mum worried.

Phone calls ignored.

A secret they all wanted to keep from me.

The pieces fit perfectly, and I shook my head in disbelief, my eyes misting rapidly as my lip trembled. *No! This can't be happening. It's got to be a joke! He wouldn't do this to me! No!*

Chapter Four

"Oww! Ouch! Mum, could you ease up? You're bruising me!"
I snapped, glaring at my mum, all the while freaking out as
I watched blood trickle down my knee.

"You can't bruise when you're already bleeding," my mum
rolled her eyes. "And it's your own fault you rushed out of that bus
without looking where you were stepping. Well, at least I'm proud
to say those part of your genes are from your dad."

I flinched and glanced out the window, my thoughts focusing
on how a day I'd thought would be perfect turned out to be the
worst in my life. The first thing I'd done after hearing my dad was
a Muslim, which is the last thing any girl in my situation would
want to hear, was *freak out*. Mum's always telling me to think
things through but somehow I never tend to listen. At the first
red light, I leaped out of the car, leaving my shocked dad staring
behind me. I'd run for a few minutes and then figured catching
a bus would be faster and so I did. I guess what I didn't count
on was being so engrossed in my own thoughts that I didn't look

where I was going and as Mark likes to exaggerate 'fell off a cliff' when stepping off the bus. Luckily, Mark had been waiting at the bus stop for another date of his, seeing as his car was at the mechanics. After staring at me gobsmacked for a few minutes he helped me up, a grin plastering his face. It took me quite a while to stand up as I'd scraped my knee pretty badly.

"What are you staring at?" I'd growled.

"A careless, immature, sixteen year old who likes to spend most of her time falling off buses and breaking her bones."

"Yes, that's quite obvious…but why are you smiling?" I replied, irritated, brushing dirt off of myself.

"Because I knew this was going to happen. You're too predictable. Or maybe I'm just really talented…" he said, bragging and already on a roll.

"At reading people's faces or on knowing what they're going to do next?" I grinned, elbowing him so hard that he tripped onto the stony pavement. "Bet you didn't know that was coming."

"Yeah, but what I *did* know was that you wouldn't take Dad's news lightly," he smirked, standing up and brushing his shirt clean. "And what I *did* know was that you'd overreact more than me," he continued, taking me by the arm again, this time more forcefully.

"I got it," I'd said coldly, bringing an end to the conversation. The rest of the walk home I had focused on whether I should tell Jayne and Jeff that my father had become Muslim and came to the decision that for the meantime I'd leave it be.

When my mum saw us coming, she'd swiftly led me to a couch

and started to examine my cut. Although she had no experience whatsoever in dealing with situations like these, she'd calmly laid me down and started to clean the cut, dabbing an alcohol swab on it lightly. I'd winced and squeezed my eyes shut, answering her questions on how I'd come back and specifically how I'd hurt my leg to which she'd laughed softly. She didn't ask me why I'd come back and I didn't tell her. Then she'd started insanely massaging my knee, a sign of her cluelessness when it came to playing nurse, bringing us to the present situation.

"Hey, stop! What do you think you're doing?" my mum exclaimed as I lifted myself up into a sitting position.

"I want to go to bed."

"But it's only six o'clock! And it's a weekend."

"Yeah, I know, but I've got a nasty head-ache and you have no idea how tiring today was," I whined.

"Oh, well, fine then," she said, "just let me help you up the stairs." Catching hold of my arm, she slung it around her shoulder, and shuffled me in the direction of the stairs. "You know, as much as you must hate your dad at the moment, you should know that he really cares for you and loves you."

"I don't want to talk about it," I muttered, pinching my lips together.

"He's been calling non-stop ever since you bounded out of his car like that, Katie. That was a really silly thing to do and if I didn't understand how emotionally distraught you are right now, I'd probably whack you."

I turned towards her as we reached my bedroom door, "Actually, Mum, I took all the necessary precautions. I waited till the traffic light was red, I looked to my right and left before crossing the street, I didn't speak to any strangers, I—"

Now she did whack me, on the arm, as I laughingly fled into my room. Wincing suddenly at the shooting pain in my leg, I limped slowly towards my bed and tucked myself in. Staring at my bedroom ceiling, thoughts of the day's events flooded my mind as I wondered how everything could have gone so wrong in such little time. I knew without a doubt, that whether I accepted my dad or not, my life would never be the same. I found it hard to understand that someone as exciting and entertaining as my dad would want to turn his world upside down, not just his *but mine* and Mark's too. Tears streamed down my face as I hugged myself and thought about the last weekend I'd spent with him.

"You're doing it wrong, Katie. Paddle to the right! No! Not so fast!" my dad cried anxiously from behind me.

"Well, whose fault is that?" I huffed, trying to recall why exactly I'd agreed to go canoeing with him. Oh yeah, maybe it was because of his remarkable persuasive skills.

"You're splashing me!" he yelped as I accidentally soaked his brand-new Gap shorts.

"Okay, look. Firstly, it was your genius idea to take me canoeing at five in the morning to this secluded Lake Waka-what's-its-name—"

He coughed, "Wakaboogie."

"Whatever, Wakabooger, and secondly—" I started to turn around to face him when suddenly he shouted, "Don't do that!"

TOO LATE!

The next thing I knew we were both flailing in the water, eyes wide, scared out of our minds.

"D..Dad? Are there...any sharks in here?" I asked frantically, my head bobbing in and out of the water as I repeatedly gulped in more air.

"N...no! Well, maybe," he replied as his eyes met mine.

"Crap!" I said, as I lunged into free-style and swam to the over-turned canoe. My dad of course had already reached it and was turning it over to help me get back in. I swiftly climbed in and then turned around to find that he'd disappeared.

"Dad! Dad?! Oh God, please don't let him get eaten by sharks. Please, I'll do anything. Oh God, oh God, please!" I begged as I looked back into the deep blue water, my eyes threating to fill with tears.

"Wow, you're as gullible as your mother," my dad chuckled from behind me. I shrieked as I heard his voice, and spun around. Sheesh, where'd he come from? I didn't have to squint to see how big a grin he had. I smiled at him with big, teary eyes, "You're alive."

"You didn't really think I was gone, did you? And were you just praying?!" he exclaimed as his chuckling grew louder.

"Maybe," I replied, turning red but inwardly feeling very relieved.

His mouth twitched, "My little girl is afraid of sharks."

"Terrified," I grinned, realizing the humour in it all.

He continued to laugh as he pulled me into a tight hug.

No, Dad, I was afraid of losing you, I thought, as he paddled us back to shore and held onto me all the way.

I knew from this memory that my dad would do anything for me, if that meant teaching me to canoe or helping me to master my failing cooking skills, if it meant he had to wake up two hours earlier than his normal routine to drop me off at school after a long weekend of fun or if it meant skipping work to help me finish my science project. There was nothing he wouldn't do for me. And that's why I sobbed helplessly, racking my brain, worrying for hours and trying my best to figure out why he'd become Muslim.

I know from experience that trying to convince your parents of something is normally an endless, windy path that leads you nowhere. While on the other hand, their one word can leave you in a helpless muddle, in other words you listen to them. Now, I'm not saying I've never convinced my parents of something, quite frankly I'm far from being an amateur.

"Mum, you cannot expect me to go out with a knee this...*ugly*."

"It's not ugly."

"Oh, would you rather call it pretty then? Or let's try gorgeous? My beautiful, bloody, scraped up knee is gonna turn so many heads," I replied sarcastically, early Monday morning.

"Honey, there is an invention these days called *jeans*. Dr Sanders said it would be totally fine for you to walk around in a couple of days, and you are. Or was it my imagination when I saw you jumping on Mark for the TV remote?" she asked, raising her eyebrows.

"That's beside the point. Nobody wears jeans in the summer, Mum. I mean, come on. Last time Angela McCarthy did that, nobody spoke to her for a week. And she's not even front row material."

"Then wear trousers or a dress or dungarees! You know shorts aren't the only clothing available these days."

"Yes, but they *are* the only suitable thing to wear in the summer. And I don't have any long dresses," I sulked.

"Borrow mine."

"You're a size bigger than me."

"In other words, I'm normal and you're anorexic."

"Please, don't start on that again."

"Fine, what about Capris? There's nothing wrong with that."

"Bingo! Perfect. Okay, I'll go try some on. Oh, and by the way

I know you wanted me to do some healthy walking around and all but can you *please* drop me off at Jeff and Jayne's first?" I asked, leaping up and already making my way up the stairs.

"Oh, you really are hopeless. All right then."

Chapter Five

"Jayne! This is the last time I'm calling you!" Jeff hollered from bellow the winding stairs at the Collins' beautiful seven bedroom manor. I'd been here a million times before but I still couldn't help falling impossibly in love with it a bit more. I mean who wouldn't?

From the outside it looked like any other large Notting Hill mansion with its Holiday Inn look-alike pool and humungous driveway. But on the inside, it was magical. Unlike the mostly Ikea furnished house I lived in; it had been stylishly designed by Jayne's interior-decorator mum, Cassie Collins. Every room had been tailored to provide just the right amount of luxury and glamour combined with a lived-in effect. Their living room on the ground floor was by far my favourite room with its sink-in cream, leather sofas, and exotic cultural art that dotted every inch of their ceiling, from the bright sari materials to the beautifully painted Turkish tiles, their exquisitely hand-painted walls were embellished with striking paintings from the likes of Monet and Pissarro, and their flat screen LED TV was surrounded by the latest Alexandria X-2 sound system. Not only that, but the room opened up into their garden, filled with blooming orchids, pansies and roses specifically imported from Romania and what would cause nothing less than a heart attack if Mrs Willow ever laid eyes on it. And then there was their kitchen. The ultimate show-stopper. Let's not even start there. Needless to say, countless magazines had been competing for months to get a look into the house of the woman whose clients ranged from famous tennis players to A-list celebrities.

"What's she doing up there anyway?" I chuckled, rubbing my favourite Siamese cat, Mittens, behind the ears.

I'd reached the Collins' house half an hour ago, finding Jeff hurriedly eating breakfast and Jayne still asleep. I'd smiled and told Jeff that his surprise was actually something I was getting used to now and he'd laughingly assured me that this wasn't it. Since then I'd gobbled down a pack of Doritos Jeff handed me and played ring-a-ring-a-roses with the five-year old triplets, Jamie, Lilly Anne, and Daisy.

To my surprise, Jeff started towards the door, brushing his light chestnut brown hair to the side. He was muttering to himself when he looked up and flashed his stunning jade eyes at me. He just looked at me for a moment and then shot me a half smile as he ducked his head and swiftly put on his Adidas trainers, entering the security code to the front-door.

"Where are you going?"

"We're leaving her. I told her a billion times yesterday to…"

"Be up and ready by the time the sun comes out blah blah blah," Jayne answered, as she rushed down the stairs and pulled me into a hug. She smelt like a wonderful aroma of fruits, having just gotten out of the shower and her glorious auburn hair was somehow already dry and naturally curling down to her back. "Long time, Kay."

"Five days too long for you?" I joked, linking arms with her and following Jeff outside.

"Hey, guess what?!" she suddenly shrieked, turning to me, her tawny eyes shimmering in the sunlight.

"What? I already know about the car. Oh yeah, Jeff? Are we taking that baby out for a ride or what?"

"I saw the most amazing Viviana dress at Dorothy Perkins yesterday for *less than seven pounds,*" she said, whispering the last part for emphasis. "And guess how much it was *before* the sale?"

The thing I love about Jayne is that she doesn't care what stores she buys from as long as they've got sales, and she's just brilliant at scoping out where the next sale is going to be. It's not that she doesn't buy from top stores like Gucci or Ralph Lauren, they being her favourite stores in London, but she sure won't ditch a 75% sale at Dorothy Perkins for a 15% sale at John Lewis.

"Umm...fifteen pounds?"

"Thirty-five pounds!"

"Wow."

"Look, if you guys don't hurry up, we'll never make it," Jeff muttered as we got to the end of the driveway and passed his car.

"Whoa, whoa, hold on a second," I exclaimed, backtracking in the direction of his car. "We're not taking your car, Jeff?"

"Not today. It'll take us double the time with all the traffic so we're hitching a ride on the bus," Jayne answered instead.

"Thank you *Jeff*," Jeff said wryly.

"Anytime *Jayne*," she shot back with a grin.

"Can I at least take a few moments to admire this beauty?" I asked, crouching down to peer inside.

Jeff smiled, "I'd say yes, but we really are running out of time. We're on a scheduled appointment here."

"I see," I said slowly, "so if the bus were to accidentally leave us, we'd have no option but to ride in...."

"Don't even think about it," Jeff said quickly, walking over to me and pulling me by the arm. "I promise you, you can admire it all you want later."

"All right, well, fine. I mean, it's not like it's going anywhere," I said, my eyes still trailing after it as we walked.

"No, of course not," Jeff replied, holding back an amused smile, as Jayne pulled me away from his grasp.

"And, I mean, today is the day you will try your *utter best* to impress me and of course it won't work and then I'll most probably, *no, definitely,* end up treating you two to Ben and Jerry's," I said dramatically, leaning on a sniggering Jayne and flashing a smirk at Jeff.

"So have you tried guessing yet?" Jeff asked, turning around and putting his hands at the back of his head. He sauntered backwards and lazily held his arm in the air, counting down on his fingers. "Let's see, according to you, we're taking you out to a mega-sale at Harrods, treating you to freshly-fried and seasoned salmon and crab fish at La Mer *or*…"

"*Or?*" I snorted, already knowing where this was going.

Jeff raised his eyebrows and his lips tugged up into a slow smile, "…your biggest fantasy of all. Renting all the seats at London Eye and throwing a mission impossible party."

"A mission impossible, unforgettable, outrageously unique party," I corrected, shoving him forward while trying to fight off a grin.

"Now close your eyes," Jayne said as we stepped off the bus, before I could figure out where in London we were. The entire time on the bus I'd tried catching up with Jayne on the latest sales and poked Jeff to tell me more about his dreamy car, and had completely forgotten to see where we were headed, not that it would have made much of a difference. I was the last person to ever inquire about for directions.

"Geez, you're not serious are you?" I muttered as she lay her

42

cold hands over my eyes and then attempted to walk me forward, which was not as easy as it seemed, seeing as I was a couple of inches taller than her and she had a large Marc Jacobs bag weighing her down. I could hear Jeff laughing and I groaned at the silliness of it all.

"I hope no one from school sees me, I'd be the laughing stock all year round."

"No, you wouldn't," Jayne retorted just as Jeff went, "Hold up. Is that Christy walking towards us?"

"I'm not falling for that," I muttered.

"*Katie*? Oh My God. Katie, is that you? And Jayne and Jeff? What are you guys doing here?" I suddenly heard a chirpy voice beside me.

I yanked Jayne's hands off my eyes, wondering how in the world it could be possible that I'd bump into Christy yet again. I searched around, until I heard a stifle of laughter coming from Jeff. Jayne smiled and held her hand open to him; he slapped a five pound note in it.

"I do such a superb imitation of Christy don't I, Jeff?" she sniggered, winking at him.

"Too good to be true," he replied back cheerfully, "You should've seen your face, Kay. Ah, you're so gullible."

Groaning, I mentally slapped my head and then muttered how childish their little prank was as I marched forward, head high.

"You're going the wrong way," Jeff yelled, with a hint of a laugh still in his voice.

"I don't even know where we're going!" I retaliated, turning around.

Jayne smiled, as she strolled over to me and tied an orange bandana, she'd fished out of her bag, over my eyes.

"We'll be there in no time at all."

"Sure, sure," I muttered back, raising my arms in the air and doing a very bad mummy impersonation.

With my eyes closed, I could very distinctly sense the area around me, the breezy summer air blowing against my face, cars zooming by and honking all the way, exotic smells hitting me one after the other, as we swiftly passed what seemed like a cinnamon shop and bakery, the mixed scent of J'adore, My insolence, and Deseo brushing my nose as a bunch of giggling girls tripped past us, birds singing in unison to a melody I couldn't get out of my head since last week or was I imagining that, the noisy, bumbling sound of a train whooshing past just two hundred yards away. I could just imagine the red and white flying past, skimming the trees, the people inside unaware of the magic it added to the city of London.

"Notting Hill Gate Library, all right we're here," Jeff said, just as I stopped for breath.

"Library?" Since when was going to the library a surprise?

"Okay, are you lot taking this off or what?" I asked, my hand reaching up to untie the bandana, just as Jayne's hand covered mine.

44

"Not yet."

"Oh stuff and bother." I grumbled.

As the door was opened, a blast of voices hit me and I immediately sparked up. We walked a few steps forward and the voices immediately dropped.

"Let's take a break!" I heard a deep manly voice yell and my eyebrows furrowed in confusion.

"So this is the special girl, eh?" the same voice asked, approaching us.

"The one and only," Jeff replied with a hint of a smile in his voice.

The bandana slipped away from my eyes, and as I blinked trying to adjust to the light, I found myself looking at…

"No. Oh My God, it can't be," I half-whispered, eyes growing wide as I stared at my favourite writer/screenwriter of all time.

"I can't believe it either," Nick Tayler joked, shaking my hand and smiling at Jeff and Jayne. "You were just in the nick of time; we were just about wrapping up. So I don't know about you but I'm starving, let me take you all out to lunch."

"I can't believe I got to meet *the* Nick Tayler!" I gushed as we left Mango Tree two hours later, rain pouring down on us.

"I didn't know there was more than one," Jeff joked, yanking his umbrella open, and holding it over my head.

"I can't believe he gave us each a *Mega Tayler Package Deal* for free! It has bookmarks, free movies and exclusive interviews of Vivienne Ricci and Alex Moretti. Altogether that could be worth £50!" Jayne said excitedly, shielding herself with her own umbrella.

"I can't believe how speechless I was when I saw him," I flushed.

"Beats Ben and Jerry's don't you think, Kay?" Jeff grinned, distracting me.

I laughed, "Anytime."

I couldn't stop smiling as we raced to the bus stop.

Chapter Six

"So Jayne's uncle is Nick Tayler's best friend?" Mark asked at the breakfast table the next morning. It was early Tuesday and my mum wasn't awake yet, her job as a top hairdresser at a classy hair salon on Knightsbridge didn't require her to come in everyday, for which she was beyond gracious and tactfully slept in instead. Thankfully, she'd given up on convincing me to eat more, so we were helping ourselves to heaped bowls of Nesquick and burnt toast.

"Yup."

"So he took you lot out for lunch?"

"Right again."

"And you think you might have a chance at becoming his protégé or something," he declared, fighting back a smile.

"You said it, not me. But who said miracles don't happen?" I asked, with a sly smile.

According to Jeff, it hadn't been planned at all; his uncle had visited from Los Angeles after a year and as they discussed the latest movies he'd been directing, he had happened to mention Nick Tayler. After seeing how enthusiastic they were about getting to meet him, he called him up and things, well, just fell into place.

"So, talking about miracles, what do you think of Dad's?" Mark asked, clearing his throat.

So now he was ready to talk about it. I thought about it, *what was my opinion at this point?* I'd decided a while ago that avoiding him would be the best option, unless I wanted to get hurt, which I really didn't. I mean, this was one of my most important years in school, I had a reputation to take care of, and I certainly didn't want to be remembered as 'the girl whose father became Muslim'.

"I don't know, man. I'm just so confused."

"Yeah, it was like that for me too."

"*Was?*"

"Yeah, in the beginning," he said, his fingers combing through his blonde hair. "I didn't have anyone to talk to, and I knew I wasn't supposed to tell you, even though believe me sometimes I was so close to letting it out. And then I tried to avoid him."

My eyebrows rose as I thought of this, not that it wasn't expected, but even the thought of Mark and Dad not teasing me together was a bit strange. But I guess that's how it was now.

"Yeah and you're still sticking to it, right?"

"Nope," he replied cheerfully, and I realized it had been a few weeks since I'd seen him this happy.

"What do you mean?" I asked, irritated.

"Look, haven't you noticed in the past few weeks how I've been eating lunch every day at Ringo's?"

"Yeah," I replied, wondering how in the world that had anything to do with my question.

"Well, it all started out with me strolling into Ringo's one day. I went because Charlie rung me up and told me they were serving my favourite, I thought it a bit odd that he'd actually taken the time to call me but once I got there and saw Dad, I realized I'd been set up and was all for walking out but...but Dad just had this look, this *pleading* look, on his face and so I scraped out a chair and listened to him. I was there for half an hour, and their set-up had some truth to it because they did serve my favourite."

"W…wait. You sat with Dad?"

"Yeah. Come on, it can't be that hard to believe."

I just looked at him.

"Okay, fine, so this past month I've been giving him the shoulder but….things change, Kay. People move on. I've moved on."

"*How?* Did he plead with you and beg you to –" I started off, disgust apparent in my voice.

"No, no, it wasn't like that," he waved his hand, "we just talked everything out. I told him I needed more time to think it all through, so he suggested we meet up every day for lunch. Slowly, slowly, I began to accept him, you know Dad just has this certain persuasiveness in him, but I made it completely clear to him that from now on we don't discuss, you know...err...Islam, and we just start off where we left things —"

"Whoa. Slow down. So you just forgave him?"

"Yeah, I'd been mulling it over for quite some time and after meeting him like that for a few days, I just made up my mind. I mean, Kay, I don't care whether he wants to dye his hair pink or join the army, that's his personal choice. So why should being a Muslim matter that much? It's not like we ever practiced Christianity before. All I want is for things to go back to normal like they were before."

"Look, I don't want to burst your bubble or anything but things won't ever *be* normal again," I replied acidly.

"Yes, they will. Well, as normal as skimmed milk is to a cat," he laughed.

"Huh?"

"Look Kay, have you even thought of Dad in this? His whole life has changed. I mean, firstly he has to learn about this whole religion he just embraced and live up to it, and change his lifestyle. Some of his friends have deserted him, and to top it all off? His kids, who he practically lives for, have stopped returning his calls and can't even look him in the face," Mark fumed right at the end.

"Hey, Dad brought this on himself, okay? Don't lecture me about what's right, Mark. When did Dad think about that? When his friends 'deserted him'? Or when his life fell apart?" My voice grew louder, and my cheeks felt hot with anger.

"*When did Dad think what's right?* Katie, when was the last time we made a mistake and Dad fixed it all up? Are you counting even the billion times he stood up for us? Put them next to this one decision that Dad made, and that Dad believes in and then see. Look at yourself, Katie, you're Dad's mirror image and don't think for one second that that's all he's given you."

Tears gathered in my eyes, threatening to spill, as I listened to his words but I still felt I had to fight back. This wasn't my fault, this wasn't my fight.

"I may look like Dad but that doesn't mean I'm going to go become like him, become some kind of *Muslim,*" I retorted, as if the word was a blasphemy, "and let my life fall apart."

"So is that what's really bothering you? Or is it the inconsequential fact that you, Katie Anderson, might lose a few snotty friends of yours? That your Queen Bee status might be at risk?"

"*How dare you?*" I glowered, gritting my teeth, hot tears pouring down my face now. "Dad goes away for six months in which I count every day till he comes back and then he tells me he's M—" I stopped for a second and sucked in my breath, slowly letting it out. "He's changed, and expects me to accept it just like that, with absolutely no regard to the fact that this is one of my toughest years in school, I've never even heard of Muslims except that every news channel believes them to be terrorists, and you think *I'm the one being selfish?* All that man did for me finished when he became Muslim," I spat.

Tearing a tissue from the tissue box, I furiously wiped at my tears and turned my head to look out the window. Still shaking with emotion, I tried to focus my eyes on what was outside and suddenly noticed that it was raining. As my tears dried, I realized that the rain was a reflection of the aching in my heart, and wondered when the sun would come out again.

Mark sighed, "Look, I didn't start on this whole topic to upset you. I'm sorry. But Kay, don't you think you're being a whole lot judgmental? He's been your dad for sixteen years and a Muslim for three months."

With barely a glance in his direction, I spoke coldly, "I don't want to talk about it."

Well, tough, I wasn't just going to forget about it all in the clap of a hand or something. Yeah, he'd been my dad for longer than he'd been Muslim but change always has consequences, and for this change, it was me.

"So," Jayne said, "school starts in exactly five days. What do you wanna do?"

As I lounged in her room, staring up at the white ceiling, my eyes following the dancing pink rays reflecting off her vibrant fuchsia walls, I sighed softly.

"Hmm…I don't know. Just stay here and die slowly."

She laughed, "Kay, what's on your mind? You seem so out of it lately."

I held my tongue, not wanting to ruin the day by getting too emotional.

"Look I can tell from your face that you've got something bothering you. Now you tell me, Katie Anderson, or expect a mega pillow beating," she threatened, switching off her TV and pinching my side.

I winced. "It's my Dad."

"Oh," she looked confused, "I didn't expect that. Normally you only bring your dad up when he *solves* the problem."

"This time he is the problem."

"All right then, tell me what it is and I'll see what I can do," she said, her eyes twinkling mischievously as she punched her open palm.

"Jayne, you couldn't hurt a fly, least of all my dad, whom by the way you adore."

"I know," she smiled sheepishly, "Who wouldn't adore a dad who spoils you with gifts, ranging from ski trips to movie nights, every other week? And you know I'm not talking about gifts per se, it's the whole I-want-to-spend-quality-time-with-my-daughter thing."

"Ah, I don't know. It's just not that simple anymore."

"*What do you mean?* It's killing me."

"My dad's changed. He's not the same," I said slowly, and then after a few more seconds of painful silence I whispered, "He's become *Muslim*."

Jayne's eyes widened, "Whoa!"

"See? See, I knew you'd say that!" I cried, pointing at her.

"No, no," she raised her hands, "I mean like 'whoa, that's shocking' not 'whoa, that's a bad thing'. They're completely different."

I narrowed my eyes, "And?"

"What?"

"*What?* What do you mean what?"

"I'm just saying it's not that big a deal."

"*It's not that big a deal?!*"

"Why do you keep repeating everything I say?" she asked in annoyance.

I stared at her for a few minutes, trying to absorb what she'd just said. "Jayne, he's become *Muslim*," I repeated slowly, making sure she hadn't heard me wrong.

"Now you're repeating what you just said," she replied back

slowly, as if speaking to a child, "Are you sure you're not catching something viral? Here, let me check."

I leaned out of her reach, "So you don't care?"

"Why would I care? *Why would you care?*"

I ignored the second part of her question and instead answered the first. "Because you'd have to be seen with a girl whose father became Muslim."

"*So what?*"

Before I could open my mouth to retaliate, she added, "Look, Kay, if I told you my dad had become Buddhist, what would you say? I mean, would you worry about being seen with *me*?"

"No, of course not. That's silly—"

"Exactly."

"—because your dad hasn't become Buddhist, has he?" I countered.

She giggled, breaking the tension instantly, "No, can you imagine him sitting in peace for even a moment without the triplets yelling for a 'piggy back' every two minutes."

My mouth twitched, "That would be something to see." After a moment's thought, I added, "But then, so would walking around with a Muslim dad."

"Kay, image isn't everything. You of all people should know that. Come on, you're the only popular girl in school who isn't

55

pressurized into having a boyfriend, the only one who isn't into yacht parties and salon makeovers *every* day, *and the only one who thinks studying is more of a priority than shopping.* Why would having a Muslim dad even matter? And even if it does, none of us could deal with it better than you will."

I could not believe this.

Jayne Collins, who believe me, was all into image was giving *me* a pep talk. And a really good one too.

"You're into image."

Her eyebrows rose in surprise, "Wow, no holding back, huh?"

I cringed uneasily, just as she shook her head, laughing, "It's alright. I knew that was coming. Look, I'm into looking good, but I've never believed that outer beauty is all that matters and you know that because you were the one who taught me that."

I sighed, "What about you? Could you deal with it?"

"No," she said, coming to sit by me on the bed.

I looked at her in astonishment. Had I heard her right? Wait, so that's it? No more late-night chats, no more emergency phone calls, no more diet planning together, no more shrieking in the school bathroom after realizing Jeff had replaced her ultra-shine hairspray with blue hair dye —

"Oh my god! I didn't shriek! That was soft screaming. And what are you talking about anyways?" Jayne exclaimed, going instantly red and shoving me off the bed.

Oops. So I'd been saying that all out loud.

"Look, I just don't get it. I mean, after all we've been through, years and years of friendship, you're just going to ditch me like that?" I asked, as I sat up.

"Huh? Oh....oh right! That's what you mean," she said as if it had just dawned upon her. She looked down at me and grinned and then slowly her shoulders started shaking as her face became a funny shade of red.

"Jayne? This isn't funny," I sniffed, to which she erupted into laughter. "Gosh, what has gotten into you? Jayne. *Jayne!*"

I watched her perfect auburn curls bounce up and down and her tawny eyes fill with tears as she tried to muffle her laughter. Her soft, creamy white skin was pulled up into a goofy grin, though still doing no harm to the face that had been asked to grace the cover of 'Vogue' last time we attended the magazine's annual award party. I stared at her, wondering if this was the last time I'd see her laugh like this.

"Oh, my stomach's killing me now. Don't ever do that to me again, Kay," she joked, wiping tears from her eyes.

It wasn't just the way she was smiling at me now that confused me, but the mere fact that she was still calling me by my the nickname she'd given me when we were five perplexed me. Wasn't she going to throw me out of her room? I folded my arms and waited for her explanation.

Her mouth pulled up into a grin again as she said, "When I said no, I meant I'd probably not be able to deal with something like that. Unlike you, I'd probably lock myself up here until God knows when, not that having a Muslim dad is that big a deal or anything... but you know the fact that I'm obviously more superficial than you," she winked at me.

"Hey, you know I wasn't being serious about that."

She waved her hand to silence me then sniggered, "*What I did not mean* was that I'd desert you for something you weren't even responsible for. What kind of friend do you think I am? You know, you really need to start paying more attention to the things around you. Eleven years of friendship isn't something I'd throw out the window, Katie Anderson," she finished, yanking me up to sit beside her, "And neither would Jeff. You're going to tell him right?"

I nodded, "I was going to tell you both today, I'd kind of planned it in my head, but he's not here, so you can tell him when he gets back. Just, please, record his reaction."

She laughed, "Sure thing."

Laying my head on her shoulder, I smiled, partly with relief and partly because I'd just had a huge burden lifted off of me. "When did long pep talks become your specialty?" I asked, nudging her.

And then the girl who was named after the famous British ice dancer, Jayne Torvill, wrapped her arms around me and said, "When weren't they?"

Chapter Seven

"Wow," I said, staring at the TV screen in front of me and trying to hold back tears.

It was the last weekend before school started and my mum had decided we sit down with a Leonardo Di Caprio movie.

"That's an understatement," my mum sighed dramatically.

"How can he be so…," I started, then looked at my mum and gasped. "Are you crying?"

"N…No! No. Just…," she wiped at her eyes vigorously, avoiding my bemused stare. I fought back a smile and raised my eyebrows, to which she swiftly said, "I…got some dust in my eyes. I don't….these…why would I…," she was getting frustrated with her own poor attempt at lying and finally huffed loudly. "Shoot me."

"Shoot *me*," I said, giggling.

She took in my teary eyes and then joined in the giggling, as we both blushed slightly and wondered why we always got so teary-eyed at the end of his movies. Maybe it was because he died in nearly every one.

"You know your dad was always jealous of him," my mum chuckled.

I knew that we would eventually talk about my dad, but it was surprising to see how often he appeared in our daily conversations. If my mum didn't bring up stories about his carelessness or Mark didn't talk endlessly about how they spent another lunch together, I'd still be thinking about him constantly. It's funny how whenever you really want to forget someone, memories keep popping up instead.

"He was?" I asked, coughing as I choked on some of the Coke I'd just been gulping down.

"Oh yeah. That's why he was totally against me naming Mark after him."

"*You wanted to name Mark after him?*" I hooted.

"But your father didn't," she grumbled jokingly. "And when he sets his mind to something he always gets what he wants. Same with you. That's why I can't help wondering who's gonna get their way this time?" she said thoughtfully to herself.

I looked down, knowing that my mum was absolutely right. Although most of the time I did get my way, like this one time I'd wanted a kitten and my dad had refused me because he feared it would eat his two-year old fish. In the end I'd persuaded him to get me one anyway and my happiness lasted for about a week, until the day I found the tail of his fish dangling out of my kitten's mouth. I remember feeling extremely anxious and upset that he'd been right even as I'd guiltily replaced the fish with a much dumber one.

Now though, the matter was different. I couldn't change the fact that my dad was Muslim, and even as I hoped with all my heart that I'd get my way this time, I couldn't help but feel that even if I did, my dad might still be right.

All of a sudden, I heard laughter approaching followed by the shrill ringing of the doorbell. Mark was home. With Dad. They'd spent a trial weekend together, seeing as Mark was warming up to him now, and apparently from the looks of it, he wasn't bolting from the car like I last had but actually seemed to be enjoying himself.

"That's probably Mark. You want me to…," my mum started, her incomplete question answered with a vigorous nod.

My eyes followed her as she opened the front door, allowing only Mark in and politely informing my Dad that I still didn't want to see him. He didn't protest and instead left with a 'Just tell her I love her' line, which for some odd reason irritated me. He hadn't even tried to talk to me. I'd expected he'd at least plead or beg to see me.

I looked on as my mum shut the door and then came to sit by me, gently laying my head on her lap as her fingers played with my hair. Mark waved a quick hello before trotting upstairs, and I turned my head before he could notice my tear-stained face. Tears streaming down my face, I fought the many thoughts that had for the past few days been giving me a throbbing head-ache. All focused around one question, *Why?*

"I'm so exhausted," I sobbed, cuddling in to her.

"It'll all be over soon, honey. Just give it some more time," she said soothingly, rubbing my back gently and beginning to sing softly. In that moment, I felt like a child again, remembering how she'd do this every now and then when a pet died or a friend moved away. Consoled with these thoughts, I let my worries drift away with the rhythm of her singing, my eyes growing heavier and heavier as her gentle humming grew softer and softer.

"Mo-om! Where'd you put that shirt I bought from Dior last week? I can't find it!" I yelled at the top of my lungs as I frantically emptied yet another shopping bag onto my bedroom floor.

School was re-opening today after a long two week mid-term break and I couldn't find a single, decent outfit to wear. Seeing as my knee was still black and blue, I'd ruled out many of the new shorts and mini-skirts I'd just bought and which just happened to make up most of my summer shopping. I scrummaged through my latest shopping, in search of a classy Dior top that I'd bought specifically for the first day back, when I realized it was nowhere to be seen.

"Mo-om!"

"It's here, it's here," she said, rushing into my room and holding up the top for me, "It got mixed up with some of my shopping bags. Don't worry, I ironed it for you."

"Oh, thanks," I replied and then politely shoved her out of my room so I could get ready.

Jayne had called ten minutes ago to tell me that she and Jeff were on their way and had just popped in at the café round the corner to pick up our daily morning lattés. They'd be here any minute and so I rushed through my usual routine, hoping I wouldn't be late. I skipped down the stairs just in time and grabbed a muffin from the kitchen top. The gentle purring of Jeff's car became louder as it slowed to a stop and after a few seconds I heard an anxious honk.

"You know you're gonna miss my car, right?" Mark stated from where he sat, munching on a chocolate muffin, "Before you know it, you'll be begging me to let you ride in it again."

I laughed loudly, "Yeah, just hold on to that thought while I jump into the Mercedes Benz parked outside."

Winking at him, I quickly slipped a multi-coloured Express scarf around my neck and shouldered my cream leather Jimmy Choo handbag.

"Last chance, Katie," he called out as I opened the front door.

I grinned as I turned towards him one last time, "I'll pass. You know, I really had no idea you were going to miss me this much."

"Pshhh. I don't miss—" he started, as I laughingly shut the door on him. Walking up to the car, I waved at the twins, whilst letting out a low whistle of appreciation.

"I am so lucky to ride in this."

"You bet," Jeff grinned, then tilted his head to the backseat where Jayne, dressed head to toe in Chanel, and as always looking incredible, had made herself comfortable.

I carefully seated myself on the plush white seats and grinned at Jayne who immediately gave me a quick once-over.

"Don't you look good."

"First day rule: Look good or don't bother coming."

"I'm guessing you got that from Christy?" Jeff asked dryly.

"No, Jeff, from you. Of course I got it from her," I chuckled.

"Well, rules are meant to be broken."

"In your world."

"My world is this world."

"Oh right, so then mine is heaven?" I joked, to which he just groaned.

"Earth to the both of you! Aren't we running a little too early? Let's take a detour, how about French Connection?" Jayne asked, her eyes glinting.

"No way," Jeff retorted, "It's good to be early."

"Sometimes I wonder if he's adopted," Jayne stated solemnly, turning towards me.

"Could be… maybe he's secretly some mob boss's son," I teased.

"Which would make me filthy rich," Jeff smirked.

"Or a gang thief's."

"And clever."

"Or a terrorist mastermind's."

"And famous."

"Or a psychotic butcher's."

"And muscular," he wagged his eyebrows.

"How about the son of a poor, lonely farmer…from China?" I huffed, rolling my eyes.

"*That* would make me someone with hope."

"Or despair."

"Would you guys zip it? I'm sure this bantering of yours must be highly entertaining to the both of you, but it's seriously not helping my growing headache," Jayne growled.

"Of course, Master," Jeff said cheerfully.

"Sensei," I sniggered.

"Teacher of all that is good and bad."

"Professor of happiness."

"We're here!" Jayne exclaimed with sudden relief.

I looked up just as the car abruptly stilled to a halt and Jeff switched the engine off. Stepping out and shielding my eyes from the sun, I gazed spellbindingly at the glorious, one-and-only Le Fevre High School in front of me and instantly my mind felt at ease; all the recent problems that had swum dizzy circles in my mind were now being slowly drowned out. This school was like home to me, I'd spent some of the best moments of my life making memories here and had long before blocked out thoughts of ever leaving it. I treasured walking through the endless corridors when they were empty and sitting on the cold bleachers in the football field on a rainy day, I relished my time in front of the revolving mirrors in the bathrooms, whilst chatting with classmates early in the morning and delaying going to class by just a tad bit more, I savoured the feeling of dangling my legs into the turquoise, heated swimming pool as I watched the reflections of students passing by, and I absolutely loved the dining hall where you could find all varieties of food being served, from Scandinavian appetizers to Russian soup, and Indian rice to Brazilian Chicken, making you feel like you were in a different country altogether.

"That last one was pretty good," Jeff whispered into my ear.

"Am I hearing this right? Is Jeff Collins complimenting me? Has the world just turned upside down?" I asked playfully, eyebrows raised.

"That would be your world," he winked.

For a long millisecond I felt this strange warmth fill me, as if that wink had meant something, but quickly brushed it away. Strangely enough, these long milliseconds were becoming uncannily common, like when I'd see Jeff with someone from school and his playful, annoying demeanour would turn into something more charming and enigmatic, or when he'd be addressing the school as a respected senior and captain of the football team, but most of the time when I'd hear girls' whisper about his ever so dashing smile and deep jade eyes that he'd inherited from his mother.

"Come on, Kay. What are you waiting for?" Jayne asked impatiently, pulling me out of my trance and back to the throngs of students around me. "I know you can't wait for Max Swift to lay his eyes on you," she teased before hauling me into the school.

I turned one last time and waved at Jeff, who was instantaneously surrounded by his football team, but still staring at me, with an undeniably annoyed expression on his face.

"Oh, please. That would be the last thing I'd want. I just wish this year he's got eyes for someone else," I muttered as a smirking Jayne sauntered off to her Spanish class.

Just then I heard a giggle beside me and turned to find myself looking at my favourite French classmate, Sophie Chevalier. She shot me an infectious grin and asked teasingly, "Do I hear someone complaining about being the centre of Max Swift's attention?"

"Oh yeah, big time," I said, grinning back.

I looked her over and was once again astounded by the magical charisma she exerted. Her shoulder-length jet black hair curved softly around her face enhancing the large, playful apple eyes that were smiling up at me, and with not a trace of makeup on her cheerful, diamond-shaped face, she still managed to look like she'd just stepped off of a magazine photo-shoot. She was wearing black skinny jeans and a stylish Dolce and Gabbana white top, and I laughed knowingly as I eyed her trademark over-indulgence in accessories that lined her arms and neck.

"What?"

"Aren't you missing a bracelet or two on that arm?" I teased.

"No, I'm pretty sure I….very funny," she narrowed her eyes at me.

"Oh, but I could've sworn that arm looked heavier than the other," I cocked my head to the side.

She threw her head back and laughed, "Oh, I missed you, Katie Anderson."

"I missed you too, Soph," I winked at her.

Laying my arm lazily on her shoulder, which was level to my rib cage due to her wheelchair, we disappeared into the sunlit, crowded hallway.

Chapter Eight

"So what will it be today?" the waiter asked, as we sat in the glamorous school dining hall. Last years polished bloob tables and stools were now replaced by round fire-truck red sofas, the walls highlighted with swirling shades of hot pink, red zinc, neon yellow and fiery orange and the tables made of reflecting, crystal glass.

I turned to Jayne and asked, "The usual?"

"Oh no, I've got to check out the new menus," she exclaimed, rubbing her hands together.

I chuckled and then politely ordered for me and Sophie, "Fresh orange juice, Caesar salad for me and a garden salad for her, and the Lebanese grilled chicken special with hummus on the side."

As Jayne began her order, Christy and a few of her friends came over and seated themselves beside us.

"Hey, girls. Had a nice holiday?" I asked politely, taking in the bronze tan and fancy new haircuts that most of them were sporting now.

"Only the best," Eva Parker gushed, flipping her hair over her shoulder and smiling widely, her newly whitened teeth sparkling in the sunlight.

"I'm getting the feeling she says that for every vacation now," Jayne muttered to me before turning to Eva and inquiring on where she'd travelled.

"Skiing in Aspen and then we vacationed for twelve long days in Montana. The Americans just couldn't get enough of my British accent," she smirked.

Christy, in the meantime, was scrutinizing the new menu, and Sarah was muttering to herself as she calculated how many calories she would allow herself to eat for lunch.

"Sounds fun," Sophie beamed. "I went to Paris for a week to spend some time with my grand-mère and then spent the rest of my vacation here, bored out of my mind as the doctors tried some more treatments," she laughed enthusiastically, her French accent slightly stronger than before.

Eva instantly shot her a sympathetic smile but as she started to open her mouth to speak, I quickly interrupted, "What about you, Sarah?"

Sarah Kaniz is the only one of us who is not European. Currently modelling for Tommy Hilfiger, she is best known for her exotic Asian-shaped blue eyes that she inherited from her Russian-Uzbekistani father and glossy black mane from her Mexican mother. She's been best friends with Christy for as long as I've known her, a smile constantly imprinted on her dainty face. If there ever was someone that could be described as Christy's complete opposite, it would be Sarah, though the one thing that's always made her stand out most is the fact that she's part Muslim, from her father's side, something she tries hard not to publicize.

"Terrific! We explored the western side of Uzbekistan this time and I swear to you I have never seen better scenery in all my life. It was so panoramic and picturesque, and the kids had such a laugh," she beamed at me, as she continued chatting about her large, boisterous family.

"The only down side was that she was apart from Zack for so long," Christy interrupted teasingly.

For the briefest of moments, I thought I saw Sarah look away uneasily, but then it was gone just as fleetingly and she was smiling radiantly again, "Yeah, I missed him so much."

"Well the fact that he missed you more should be enough to make that down side up, don't you think?" Christy winked at her, just as the waiter arrived with our orders.

"'Course," she giggled but then suddenly straightened up and I could have sworn I saw her checking herself out in the glass of freshly-squeezed orange juice placed in front of her. Immediately the other slouching girls sat up and started tucking fly away hairs to the side and rubbing their lips together, all the while staring into the clear crystal glasses before them. Oh boy, someone was coming up to the table from behind me and somehow had all these gorgeous girls flustered, besides Jayne, who was watching them with a slightly amused grin.

Assuming it was Max Swift, the bulky and incredibly self-centred jock who just happened to insist on following me around even though it was obvious most of the girls at my table would swoon if they were in my place, I barely turned my head as

71

I sighed, "Hello, Max."

"Last time I checked my name was Jeff."

I instantly narrowed my eyes and stared into my orange juice glass, realizing quickly that it served as a superb mirror, to find two glittering jade eyes locked on mine. I spun around with a wide grin on my face, "Thank God."

Jeff, who was standing right behind me, his arm placed casually on the smooth leather sofa, nodded at the many gorgeous girls at the table and muttered, "I wouldn't be that thankful."

As I raised an eyebrow questioningly, I heard a loud, confident, "Hello, Ladies," and again, I spun around but this time instead of grinning I was rapidly deciding on how I could slip away unnoticed.

Although Max Swift had just addressed the entire table, his eyes were on me. Forcing a smile, I asked, "Had a nice vacation, Max?"

"Could've been better but I won't complain," he answered, running his hands through his surfer blonde hair.

I groaned inwardly, and was just about to pick at the Caesar salad that had all of a sudden engrossed my thoughts, when my plate of delicious food suddenly slipped away from under my eyes.

My eyes trailed after the plate as it slowly inched its way towards my right, and then as I finally wrenched my gaze upwards, I found myself scowling at Jeff. Before I could launch into how utterly rude it was to steal someone else's food, Jeff said, "Sorry Max, but I need Katie for a moment. She promised to help me with something...*incredibly important*. Right, Kay?"

I blinked. *I did?*

"*I hope you didn't forget, Katie,*" he added in a child-like tone, his eyes telling me to go along with it.

I glanced at Jayne fleetingly, wondering if she knew what Jeff was on about, but she shrugged back to show she was as clueless as I. Great, now I'd have to improvise.

"Of course I didn't forget, *Jeff*," I spoke in a loud, clear tone, "How odd of you to think that I would have forgotten such an *important* matter," I laughed boisterously, "how incredibly… funnily odd," I continued with a wide, strained smile, as Jeff closed his eyes and massaged his temple. "Don't you think so, Jeff?"

Jeff dropped his hand, briefly eyeing me with daggers in his eyes, and then turned to the group, a charming smile immediately taking over his face. "Why, yes, Katie, you're right. How utterly," he shot me a look, "foolish of me not to remember. Shall we go then?" he asked, yanking me up from my seat.

"Wait, hold on," Max said slowly, pointing at the both of us, "What's this thing he accused you of forgetting, Katie?"

A look of annoyance crossed Jeff's face and he looked as if he was about to retort, when suddenly his expression changed. Releasing his grip on my arm, Jeff turned mockingly towards me, a faint smile playing on his lips, and said, "Yeah, Katie, why not enlighten everyone," he nodded to the group, "I'm sure everyone's curiosity is piqued by now."

My eyes grew as I realized what he'd just done. Oh no, no no no, this was completely unfair. *He* was the one who had brought it up in the first place. This could not be happening. Flicking my eyes towards Jayne, I eyed her pleadingly for help, but she shook her head, looking as if she'd erupt into laughter any minute.

"Katie?" Jeff cocked his head with a self-satisfied grin.

I threw him a death glare before turning my attention towards the confused eyes staring back at me.

"Right. Yeah. Totally. Well, umm, well, you see, the thing is, the errm...important matter is that ....Jeff and I have been working on a... umm...project together..."

"What kind of project?" Eva asked, narrowing her eyes.

"The errr...global awareness project," I spoke slowly, forming my words carefully, and trying to avoid looking at Jeff's growing grin, "for... umm bears... polar bears! Yeah, that's it."

As I spoke, I shouldered my bag and took a step backwards. Please don't ask me to explain. Please. Please.

"Polar bears?" Max asked incredulously.

Oh Bummer. "Yeah, you know. Their extinction rate is increasing.....as we speak," I declared, suddenly happy with how it had turned out.

"Whoa," Max said, mouth hanging open.

"It's all because of global warming, people. Wow, is it getting hot in here," I said fanning myself and preparing to launch into what I considered a terrific speech.

However, before I could urge people to use less hair spray

and consider driving at the speed limit instead of exceeding it, Jeff grabbed my arm again and smiled at the table, "*Exceptionally* important."

"Wait, just a moment," Christy said, standing up and immediately grabbing the attention of every eye in the dining hall. "As you all know, each term we have a 'Welcome Back' party at my place on the first day. Well, this year it's going to be different. My house isn't available at this time—" she paused for a moment as an audible gasp circulated, and I stole a glance at Jayne, to see her face equally surprised. Christy cleared her throat in annoyance and continued, "So since Eva's parents are on holiday, she'll be hosting it at her place instead."

This was, to say the least, astonishing. Each year, for as long as I could remember, we'd had every single term party at Christy's, it had become like a tradition. No one knew how to throw a party the way Christy did.

"And just so you guys don't worry, I've already had the invitations sent to your houses. Be there by eight," she smiled enigmatically.

"*Polar bears*? Are you out of your mind?" Jeff handing me my plate back, laughing as we exited the dining hall.

"What? That's all I could think of," I glared back, stopping mid-stride, "*And what in the world was that, back there, Jeff Collins?* Do you have any idea how embarrassing that was?" I half-yelled, slapping his arm, "Putting me on the spot like that and making a scene!"

"I didn't make a scene, that was all you," he grinned, and then backed away from my smacks, "Whoa, hey. Okay, okay, I partly made a scene. But it was only because you made it so tempting not to."

I scowled and folded my arms, "You're not making things any better for yourself."

"All right, fine. How does a sincere apology sound?"

"Sincere," I snorted, "yeah, right."

"I, Jeffrey Collins, the third," he made a face, "do solemnly and sincerely apologize for any actions or comments that may have offended the lovely Miss Katie Anderson, daughter of Jack Anderson," he began, as I rolled my eyes, fighting back a smile, "and beg for her forgiveness and good will in light of what just occurred. As a token of my deepest, sincerest, most heart-felt apologies, I would like to present to you," he paused, fishing out a coin from his pocket, "a donation for GAP." He smiled crookedly and placed it into my open palm, as I looked at him in confusion. "Global Awareness for Polar Bears project," he explained, and after a moment, "The 'B' is silent."

My eyes widened in recognition and I burst out laughing, "That's not funny."

"It does seem to be working though."

"You're crazy," I shook my head with a smile, "So anyways, what do you think of Christy's sudden change in plans?"

"That's not what I pulled you out of there to talk about," Jeff replied, his tone changing instantly.

"Oh, right, yes, the 'important matter'," I connoted with my fingers jokingly.

"I'm being serious, Katie," he stated, his expression one of sombre, and suddenly I could see that he wasn't joking anymore.

"Okay, so what's the big deal?"

He paused uncertainly, "Jayne told me about your dad becoming —"

"Shhh! Don't say it," I interrupted him, conscious of the eavesdropping ears around us.

"So that's how it is now?" he asked, raising his eyebrows.

"Excuse me?"

"You're so revolted by them that you can't even speak about them? It's funny because I really didn't expect that from someone like you."

I stood there, gaping and at a total loss for words. Moments ago, he'd been lightly joking around with me and now, all of a sudden, he was rebuking me. I had expected some sort of comfort or sympathy from Jeff, not this.

"Why is it that nobody understands my point of view?" I asked with exasperation.

"Because you're too stubborn to listen to someone else's," he replied flatly, then immediately looked like he wanted to take it back.

"*What is up with you?* We…I…we are not having this conversation," I declared vehemently, whipping around to leave.

"Katie, you know I didn't mean that," Jeff replied, quickly grabbing me by the arm and pulling me back.

I shook his arm off and retorted, "No, actually, I don't. Please, Jeff, *enlighten* me as to what you actually mean."

He cringed uneasily, "Look, all I'm saying is that….that you're making a big mistake, Kay. You're…you're blinded by anger and hurt and you're directing it all in the wrong direction. You're acting childishly."

I sucked in a sharp breath. Staring at him in disbelief, a mixture of hurt and betrayal flitting across my face, I lunged away from him. He opened his mouth and then closed it, as if not sure of how to continue, yet hoping to relay some sort of apology through the look of plea in his eyes.

My own eyes threatening to fill with tears, I turned away and marched off to the other side of the building, ignoring Jeff's indolent calls to come back. I didn't have to walk far before I realized where it was that I wanted to go and slinked off to the empty, football bleachers. Climbing up to the top of the bleachers, I shuffled into a corner and pulled my knees up to my chest, hugging myself tightly and letting loose my emotions, my shoulders racking with sobs. *Where had that come from? Why couldn't anyone understand what I felt? Why was Jeff, one of the few people I had known my entire life, turning against me at a time like this? What had I done to incite accusations from him?*

Unable to find answers to any of my questions, I continued to cry until I heard a familiar voice call out my name and the sound of footsteps making loud, pattering noises as they fast approached.

"Katie? Oh, Kay, are you all right?" Jayne asked, hurrying to my side and pulling me into a tight hug, as I broke down into another convulsion of sobs. She smoothed out my hair and rubbed my back softly. "He came to me and told me what happened, and he actually feels sorry."

I shook my head against her shoulder, and then lifted it up to wipe my tears away. Breathing out slowly to calm myself down, I gave her a shaky half-smile. "I don't understand…why…why is he angry? What did I do? I thought…I thought he'd understand."

"Oh, Kay, don't take it to heart. Jeff didn't mean any of it. He probably just doesn't want you to have a falling out with your dad. I mean, neither do I."

She continued to rub my back soothingly for a few minutes, as I felt myself slowly calm down.

"And it's just that sometimes he's a jerk," she stated, as an afterthought.

"No, he's not," I chuckled softly and sat up straighter, the moistness of the tears on my cheek fading slowly. "Jeff's not a jerk. He was just acting like one."

Jayne grinned, "Sounds like the same thing to me."

I laughed, getting up on my feet, "Come on, we're going to be late for class."

"Nuh-uh, we're sitting right here until you feel better."

I grinned, wiping away the remnants of any remaining tears on my cheeks. "All better. Honest. I'm fine now."

"All right, but don't think for a second that I'm not going to give Jeff a piece of my mind," she glowered as I pulled her to her feet.

"Give him whatever you want but a detailed account of me crying my eyes out. The last thing I need now is his pity."

"Of course. So hey, have you even thought of what you're going to wear to the party tonight?" she exclaimed, as I jumped expertly off the side of the bleachers, and helped her down. "I can't wait to go shopping for a new dress."

"Jayne, calm down," I grinned, knowing all too well what would happen if she was left to buy another 'new dress'. "This isn't one of those mega end-of-year parties that we go to. This is simply a welcome-back-to-school term party. So dress funky yet sophisticated," I said, as we made our way back towards the school doors.

She thought about it for a moment, "Yeah, I guess you're right. But there's nothing wrong with buying new shoes…"

"Jayne."

"And maybe some earrings…"

"Err…Jayne?"

"And you know, I really think I should at least try some dresses on…"

"Jayne. Stop. No, we're not going shopping today. You haven't worn half of the clothes in your closet and I plan to do something about. I'll ring up my mum and tell her I'm getting ready at your place and then we can get you sorted out," I chuckled, gripping her by the shoulders.

"Oh. Well, okay. Just don't forget our tradition," she winked.

"Dropping by at her hair salon and going wild?" I grinned, pushing open the door.

"You bet."

She looped her arm in mine and we started down the hallway as the bell rang to signal the end of the lunch break.

Chapter Nine

"Sam, style their hair, Kitty start on the make-up, and Amy get me some coffee," my mum smirked at me as she issued out orders. "Aren't I the best?"

I just laughed as I looked around at the hair salon my mum had started eleven years ago, admiring the brightly coloured walls that she had happily decided we would all paint together. I still remembered the day as if it was yesterday, the memory one of many that I hoped to always hold onto. My mum had insisted we all drive down to redecorate the old, washed-out restaurant on Knightsbridge that she had just recently purchased and converted into a salon, saying that she wanted it to have a personal touch to it, which is exactly what it got. Mark's grimy handprints lined the bottom left of the wall I was facing, the yellow butterflies I had attempted to make covered the other side. My mum's signature 'Elle' had been painted in slanting cursive just beside the 'Jack' that she'd playfully forced my dad to sign. Anyone who laid eyes on the walls would be able to notice the loving bond that had held our family then as we'd splattered paint on the walls, my dad's hands on my waist as he held me up to make some pink hearts on the ceiling, and Mark's 'Batman' illustrated cartoon that he'd drawn on the floor.

I heard an amused cough at my side as I was suddenly brought back to the present.

"Still gets you every time eh, Katie?" Kitty chuckled.

I grinned at her and rolled my eyes, "Yeah, I just can't get enough of those butterflies."

"Come on then, I'll start on you first," she said, leading me to my favourite couch. "So where exactly are you going?"

"Eva Parker's haunted manor for a welcome-back-to-hell bash."

"Take me with you," she joked.

I grinned, "In all seriousness though, the food's to-die-for."

"Okay, now I'm not kidding either."

"Sure, I mean if you want to be surrounded by college guys and—"

"All right, changed my mind," she said quickly, "So how high-profile is this party going to be anyways?"

"Well, don't tell Jayne...," I snickered, "...but this year, it's going to be pretty high-class."

She laughed, "I can see why you'd want to go then."

"I don't," I replied automatically, as if the feeling had been inside me all along and I'd just realized it then.

"What?"

I searched for the right words, "I've just had enough of these parties. They're all the same. I mean there must be more to life than...this," I gestured around with my hands.

She looked at me knowingly. "Yeah, I used to think that way sometimes. What the *purpose* of life is and all."

"You *did*?"

"Yeah, and I always reached a dead end. And then when my parents got rid of me and I had to find my own way around, I thought about it some more. I even started attending church to see if I could learn more," she shook her head, "You ask the people who go to church every day and they say ask the priest, then you ask him and he says 'You mustn't question God, repent child, repent for your sinful thoughts'," she grinned at me, looking as if none of this bothered her. Well, nothing ever did bother Kitty, who at the age of seventeen was kicked out of her house after dropping out of high school and ever since then resolved to do something better in her life. She'd told me her story before but never this, that the thoughts that had been going around my head recently had occupied hers a few years ago.

"Did you?"

"Of course not. I mean, I know I'm no devout Christian and all but I wasn't doing anything wrong. I wasn't questioning God, I was just trying to find my purpose in life," her smile slowly faded away as she added, "....and I wanted to know how someone like my dad could get away with putting my sister in the hospital for three weeks just by saying 'Christ sacrificed himself for my sins'," she connoted with her fingers.

I laid my hand on her arm comfortingly, and she looked at me straight in the eyes, "I don't believe in any of that, that Christian concept of salvation, that by the life, death and resurrection of Jesus, *righteous* Christians have attained salvation. No," she shook her head, "the way I see it, you do something good or bad, *you're* accountable for it. Why should someone else die for *my* sins?"

I tore my eyes away from hers, her question echoing in my head even as I itched to change the subject. "How's Laura now?"

Her expression softened as she said, "She's doing good. The kid's learnt a thing or two from me and she's finally holding her ground at the house. She wants to move in with me but she's not even sixteen yet…I was thinking about fighting her case or finding someone that would but my situation's not looking so good right now. What social service worker would agree to give *me*," she gestured mockingly at herself, "sole guardianship? I don't exactly fit the criteria."

"Oh come on, Kitty, you're being too hard on yourself. You might have been able to say that three or four years ago, but now look at yourself, you're a completely different person."

She smiled, "I guess so. I mean the past two years have been looking up, but that's all due to your mum. The first thing she said to me on that jam-packed subway at eight o'clock in the morning, two years ago, was, 'That elfin cut suits your face just perfectly. How would you like to earn some money for making others look like that?'" she mimicked her expertly, as I giggled, "she didn't even bother asking me if I'd cut it!"

I laughed, "That's mum for you. She has this brilliant knack of discovering people's talents."

"Yeah, she sure does. She took me in, showed me how a pair of scissors could change my life and then things were fine. I still wonder about my *purpose* from time to time, when things get too bad or good, but I'm here on this earth right now, I don't know why but I might as well try and enjoy it right?"

"I guess," I replied, a feeling of guilt taking over as I recalled the last conversation I'd had with my dad. I still couldn't seem to forget the compelling look in his eyes when he'd said, "*Katie, we all have a place in this world, a reason we were put here. Life isn't random, it has purpose. I found mine.*"

"Well, why are you going if you don't want to?" she asked, jolting me back to the present.

"Oh…umm, because if I don't go I might as well commit social suicide," I replied dryly. "It's the party of the century."

"Ah, it's for image then," she smiled slightly.

"Well, partly for the food as well," I quipped as she began to laugh. "All right, fine," I grimaced, "more or less. But one day I just know I'm gonna crack. This façade is getting too much for me."

She turned me around so I would face the mirror and then looked at me with determined hazel eyes, her hands firmly on the back of my chair. "One day you're gonna find answers, Katie, I just know it. And when you do, you better come and tell me."

"Okay, that's good. Yeah, just move a little bit to the right, now tilt your head. *Katie,* behave. Good, good." My mum angled her head as she took one last picture of me and Jayne.

"You know, mum I really don't get why it's such a big deal to you. I go to these parties all the time but no, you just have to get a picture in," I huffed, impatient to leave.

"It doesn't matter the occasion or the clothes but the smile on your face, and *that* is what I want to capture. So suck it up."

"Oh, Elle, did you get that off the internet? Or from one of those quote books?" Jayne asked admiringly as I spoke through gritted teeth, "Do I look like I'm smiling? Huh? *Do I look like I'm smiling?*"

My mum ignored me and instead beamed at Jayne, "Actually I made that one up."

The worst part of it all was that every one of those pictures had been displayed for all public to see, in the hair salon, beside my yellow butterflies. And it wasn't funny.

"All right mum I'll see you later. Don't wait up for me," I said dryly as I put on a pair of black Bulgari sunglasses and linked arms with Jayne.

"Have a blast," Sam winked.

With a final goodbye, we hurried onto the street, barely acknowledging the stunned stares and appreciative gasps we were getting. As we made our way towards Harrods for a quick shopping trip that Jayne had managed to convince me was absolutely necessary, Jayne sniggered, "That has to be the fifth time you've looked at that Gucci in the past hour."

I smiled and tucked away my watch, "Better?"

We reached Harrods five minutes later and as we sauntered towards the main door, I beamed at Edward, my favourite doorman and one who'd known me ever since my mum had begun treating me to regular trips there as a child. It had started out as a day's adventure when I was five and then eventually became our secret hang-out spot, where we spent hours excitedly discovering the inner magic of Harrods and swiftly making friends with every sales assistant, manager, security guard, and doorman. There was not a single employee at Harrods who was not familiar with the 'Andersons' by now.

"Edward! How's Mary doing?" I smiled, sparing a few quick minutes.

"Oh, she's happy as a bluebird, Miz Anderson, 'specially since she nailed that cleaning job on the second floor. Can't git her to shut her yap these days," he chuckled, "All thanks to you that is, if you hadn't put in a good word for 'er she'd still be sulking around like an awful, sick chicken."

I threw back my head and laughed, "Oh, it was nothing really though Eddie, and she so deserved it."

"Well, isn't that mighty sweet of you to say, Miz Anderson. And if I could just say so meself, you dolls are lookin' mighty fine today.

88

Yeah, you are," he nodded, his eyes crinkling on the sides as he smiled, "Got yourselves a tea party to go to?"

Jayne chuckled, "More like a hip-hop party."

"Right, well you birdies go on ahead, enjoy yourselves. But don't git too carried away now. I always say so meself that nowadays—"

"The young folk act like monkeys at a circus act," Jayne and I chorused, our mouths pulled up into wide grins, "we know."

"Well I…err…yeah," he mumbled, looking at the floor, "but you're not like any of 'em, Miz Anderson. No, siree, you're different, you're a special bird. You both are. So you take care of yourselves, awright?"

"We'll make sure to do that," I patted his arm gently, before turning to follow Jayne inside.

Harrods is like my second home. I know everything there is to know about it, from the fastest routes to reach the fifth floor, to the best cafés to dine at, from the staggering prices of designer bed linens, to the somewhat affordable prices of Harrods pencils, and from the secret staff-only corridors to the best chocolate served at the chocolate counter. There isn't an inch of the place that I haven't explored. And well, to Jayne it is home. Needless to say, we've both had over a dozen offers to become managerial store guides by the Managing Director, who insists on hiring us every time he meets us.

Now, Jayne made a beeline towards the Luxury Jewellery Room, pulling me by the hand before I was able to take a peek at the latest candy that graced the wondrous Candy Room. As we approached the jewellery counters, Jayne waved at a petite, blonde woman busy serving customers. The woman caught her eye and her face broke into an immediate grin, before she quickly signalled to her to give her a minute. Nodding her head, the woman continued to chat animatedly with the two customers in front of her, until both of them left a few minutes later, having added another carrier bag to the load of bags weighing their arms down.

She made her way to the girls immediately, "Score!" she pumped her fist into the air, "that's the eighth item I've sold today. Am I awesome or am I awesome?"

I raised my eyebrows, "Wow. You've been on a roll ever since you found out about the baby."

She nodded, patting her stomach happily, "I know. Pregnancy can have the oddest effects on a person. So, girls, what can I do for you two today? Or maybe I should say what can you do for me today?" she winked, "Wanna help me reach ten?"

Jayne laughed, "Well, actually, yes. Today may just be your luckiest day, Nat."

Natasha Louise Phillips's face had never looked as sublimely happy as it did at that moment. "Oh my god, I love you guys. Have I ever told you that before? I *love* you both. Richard said that whoever reaches ten gets to be 'Employee of the Month'. The benefits are out of this world! So thanks, really. I am so honoured and I would just like to say that in all my life," she began dramatically, "I have never met such amazingly –"

"Nat, we're kind of in a hurry," Jayne piped up.

"Yeah, I kind of ran out of words anyway. But you guys are

awesome. I'll just end with that; awesome. Right, so let's get shopping," she rubbed her hands gleefully.

Ten minutes later, we sauntered out of Harrods, grinning like little schoolgirls and swinging our shopping bags, with a final wave at Edward.

"Don't forget to send my regards to Jackie!" he yelled back at us.

Faltering slightly in my stepping at his mention of my dad, I nodded at him before following Jayne into the Collin's midnight blue, chauffeur-driven BMW as she said, "Joe, we're in a hurry. So step on it."

As we took off, my thoughts returned to my dad and the last time we'd spoken to each other, just seconds before I'd leaped out of the car. The incident was still instilled in my memory and yet the exact expression on my dad's face was fuzzy in my mind, and had me replaying the incident again and again just to capture it. Had it been surprise that had crossed his face? Or was it a look of pity? Or perhaps it had been guilt? But if so, then why was it that I mirrored the same feeling, why was it that every time he came to mind, I pushed thoughts of him away even as my heart ached to see him again, and why was it that on my way to the biggest party of the year, all I could think about was Islam and the effects it was having on my life.

I closed my eyes in an attempt to clear my thoughts and then opened them once more. I turned to focus my attention on Jayne, taking in the make-up and hairstyle that did little to transform her already stunning looks, and then recalled the fleeting glance that I had taken of my own reflection just before we had left the hair salon earlier. I never knew what to expect as the girls were always trying out different hairstyles and make-up techniques on me, but the empty look in my eyes was certainly something I wasn't prepared for. In that glance, I'd stared beyond the silver eye shadow and the soft curls draped around my neck, and instead focused on the eyes of a person whose life would never go back to the way it was before, a person who now understood that the thoughts that ruled their mind were going to take over and become actions, *a person who was looking for answers.*

Chapter Ten

I stepped into the cool, dark hall lit with dancing disco lights and nudged Jayne. Over the blasting music I yelled, "Do you think we're over-dressed?" as my eyes scanned the various girls around me wearing simple low-slung jeans and a top, which was a dramatic contrast to what we were wearing.

"Nuh-uh," she replied, pointing her finger towards Sarah who looked striking in a black and white mini floral dress. A delicate silver necklace adorned her neck, her glistening black hair was pulled up into a high ponytail and she wore black Balenciaga heels as she approached us just then. Her eyes widened with admiration as she got closer, a smile playing on her lips.

"You girls look fantastic!"

"Right back at you," I said, laughing softly at her expression.

"I should have come over to see you before stepping out of my house," she smiled.

"Are we the last ones to arrive?" Jayne asked.

"If you think you're late then think again. There's still a lot more to come," she winked. "Come on, I'll take you to Eva's dressing room, the girls are still getting ready."

As we followed her, my eyes fell upon the gigantic table to the side, overflowing with food and beverages, and I gasped. If it weren't for the legs of the table I wouldn't have known what colour it was, seeing as every inch of the table was covered with soda cans, cocktails, bags of crisps, exotic salads, juicy chicken wings, cheesy quesadillas and platters of pizza and pasta. It looked as if everything Eva had laid eyes on she'd bought and I silently wondered how long it had taken just to get the table ready.

"Eva doesn't seriously expect that food to run out, does she?" I squeaked.

Sarah took in my stunned expression and laughed loudly, "Like I told you, there's more to come."

As we got closer to Eva's dressing room, we heard an annoyed shriek.

"Megan! Can't you do a single thing right in your life?!"

I instantly recognized the voice as Eva's and raised my eyebrows as I walked into the room and saw Megan, a junior from my biology class, puffing and panting as she tried unsuccessfully to pull the zipper up on Eva's dress. Eva stood menacingly in front of her, her hands clutched angrily to her sides and stared at us as we entered, the anger in her eyes instantaneously transforming into jealousy. Although Eva was almost shockingly thin, the dress she'd chosen was much too tight and stuck to every inch of her body.

"I have absolutely no chance of looking as good as you two

today," she moaned, her eyes lingering on our dresses.

I looked at what we were wearing once more and shrugged, "It was all Jayne. She can do wonders when it comes to this stuff."

I was wearing a Twelfth Street metallic grey dress of sequined chainmail and draped three-quarter sleeves. The dress reached just above my knees and I'd paired silver gladiator shoes to go with it, showing off my painted silver toe-nails. I'd accessorised with feather-light white-gold earrings and an array of silver bangles to wear in place of a necklace due to the high, boat neckline.

Jayne was wearing a dazzling strapless, purple Vera dress that played up her slim figure with opaque dark grey tights. A thin, silver Ashley leather belt was wound around her waist and her bare shoulders were covered with a midnight black velvet jacket. A gorgeous violet and black choker glittered at her throat, as she chatted vivaciously with Sarah.

"But let's not chat about that right now. That dress...Eva, don't you think you could maybe...consider wearing another?" I asked as I grimaced at the single-shoulder black leather dress plastered to her body.

"Oh no, I have been spending over-time in the gym for the past few weeks to get into this dress and I am going to. Even if it kills me," she said, through gritted teeth, once again glaring at Megan.

Just then Christy sauntered out of the adjoining bathroom with a smug grin on her face. "I convinced them and so the band will be here in an hour."

"Oh my gosh! Christy, you're amazing! I'm like their number one fan!" Megan gushed, her attention immediately diverting from the task at hand.

"If you don't get that zipper up in less than thirty seconds I will make sure that you don't get within five miles of them tonight. Am I clear?" Eva spoke icily.

"Crystal," Megan replied, her face going pale.

Christy turned towards us, opening her mouth and then shutting it immediately, her face instantly registering shock. She shook her head and smiled tightly, "You girls are always surprising me."

I looked her up and down, "You've got to be joking."

I took in what she was wearing and again thought exactly that. Christy looked beautiful in a strapless midnight blue origami pleated dress with large crayon blue, white, and purple swirls decorating it. It reached just below her knees and she wore shocking blue stilettos with it. Her hair was brushed tightly away from her face and tied up into a magnificent fishtail that reached her shoulder blades, and her make-up was as flawless as usual.

She strolled towards the full-length mirror closest to her and tilted her head to the side, as if wondering if she'd gone with the right outfit. Her eyes scanned every inch of herself before she finally turned around and beamed, "So, should we get this party started?"

"About time," Jayne grinned.

I looked out at the growing crowd of people in front of me, most of them classmates, who had been dancing non-stop for the past hour, and sighed again. I couldn't find it in me to get up and sway to the music as a feeling of uneasiness enveloped me, and instead I resorted to lounging at a refreshment stand to the side, highlighted by the bright pink lights overhead. As Jayne headed for the dance floor, I decided to get a drink and ended up gulping down quite a lot of juicy cocktails. Watching the dancing bodies around me, I realized it was a mistake to come. I knew that I should have followed my gut feeling, which as soon as Christy had announced the party, had told me to stay home.

"This seat taken?"

I turned my head to see Sarah slide onto the seat next to me, not waiting for an answer, and order a smoothie for herself.

"Now it is," I smiled.

She looked at me in surprise, as if suddenly recognizing me, "Oh, Katie. I didn't see you there. It's so dark in here. What are you doing here? Why aren't you dancing with the rest?"

I shrugged, "Not really in the dancing mood. You?"

She ducked her head slightly lower, "Hiding from someone."

I chuckled, "You're kidding, right? This place is practically swamped with people and the lights are all out. It's impossible to find anyone here."

She shook her head, "Not for Zack. He could find me even if he was blind-folded," she rolled her eyes, taking a sip from her smoothie.

I furrowed my brows, "Isn't that a good thing? Last I heard you guys were going steady…"

Sarah put a hand to her head and exhaled, "I didn't invite him to the party, Christy did. Apparently, she wanted to 'surprise' me," she connoted with her fingers, "when really, all I wanted was some time to myself, for once. It's a bit too much having him around all the time."

I nodded, staring into my half-empty cocktail glass.

"And then," she added quietly, "there's the whole part about me wanting to break it off."

I lifted my head and looked at her in surprise.

"I mean," she said swiftly, "I haven't told him yet, but I've just….been thinking about it a lot lately…."

"Have you talked to anyone else about this?"

She shook her head, "No, just you," then exhaled a humourless laugh, "it's funny how I'm telling the last person on earth I'd expect to understand."

"What?" I asked, sitting up straighter in my seat. "What are you talking about?"

"You wouldn't understand."

"Just try me. Hey, come on, I wanna know," I nudged her, feeling slightly hurt at her words.

She turned to look at me, "You know, that whole thing going on between you and Jeff."

My jaw dropped open and I stared at her with wide eyes. *Had I heard her right?* Because, I was quite sure she'd just said…

"*What are you talking about?* There's nothing going on between…*Jeff* and me," I exclaimed shrilly, after finally finding my voice, "What in the world? We're *just* friends. "

"Shhh, you're too loud," she motioned with her hand and then continued, "And the fact that you don't even realize it is what makes it so special."

"Wha—"

"But see," she interjected, "me and Zack never had that, that *bond*. We're just together to pass the time."

I looked at her as if she was crazy. If she had told me that donkeys could harmoniously sing the alphabet, it would have made more sense to me than what she had just declared. *Bond?* What was she going on about?

She shook her head and whispered, "And even if we did, it's at the risk of…"

"Risk of what?" I leaned in closer, my attention momentarily altered.

She exhaled heavily, "My personal beliefs."

I furrowed my brow, "I don't understand."

She took a deep breath and turned towards me, her eyes locking onto mine as she stared at me intensely for a moment, "I'm a Muslim. So…it would be at the risk of my Islam."

I stared at her, speechless, unable to absorb what she'd just said. *Islam*. It seemed like the religion was seeping into my daily life and surrounding me everywhere I went.

In all my years of knowing Sarah, I had never once heard her use that word, *Islam*. And that too, with a possessive note in her voice. I'd always imagined that she was ashamed of her religion, that she saw it as an obstacle to attaining the popular image that she had created for herself, that it was beneath her to mention it to her non-religious friends, but I was wrong. Quite astonishingly wrong. Because the girl I saw before me was not in the least bit ashamed of her religion, from the confident challenge in her eyes to the way her shoulders were set firmly, her face passive and calm, making her look more beautiful to me in that moment than she ever had before. In fact, if there was any crack that I could detect in her composure then it was the flicker I caught in her eyes, a flicker of shame mixed with regret, but even that was quite obviously not in blame of her religion, but in blame of herself.

"What do you mean by risk?"

"In Islam, we don't date, or at least, we're not supposed to," she smiled, "It's as pure a religion as any can be. No dating, no flirting, no illicit affairs, no heart-shattering break-ups, no going out with different guys until you find the right one for yourself; the one who makes your whole world, but still opts to leave you after ten years together. None of that. It's just simple and pure marriage. Uncomplicated, unblemished, untarnished."

"Wow, I never looked at marriage that way," I uttered softly, when really I meant that I had never looked at Islam that way. Never even tried to see it from a different viewpoint or from the perspective of a Muslim. I'd always just accepted what I'd heard from people, from the news, and from the media in general. What Sarah had just spoken about shed some new light on Islam for me, and for once I was listening to things for myself instead of accepting them unthinkingly. For once, I was letting down my guard and allowing myself to think about Islam objectively.

"A lot of people don't. They see it through the eyes of the 'new generation', as a cage or trap, with too many rules and complications, when really, it's the best solution when it comes to matters of love," she proclaimed.

"So, if you believe that then…" I trailed off, a rising intonation in my voice.

"I didn't realize it until just recently, and by then I knew it was too late. I've risked so much, and wasted away so much of my life," her eyes watered, "sacrificing my Islam in the process. I'm afraid I won't get another chance. I'm a goner."

"You never know, you might still have a chance," I spoke awkwardly, unsure of what to say, "I mean, if it means so much to you, it's worth looking into, right? I mean, I don't know, you probably have—"

"No, you're right. I haven't…I…I haven't gotten to that stage yet. I guess just speaking to you out loud like this has made so many things clear for me. I know what I want to change in my life now; I just…I just hope it all works out."

I rubbed her back gently as she cried softly, "Here, take a sip of this, it'll make you feel better," I nudged the cocktail at her.

She glanced at the cocktail and shook her head, wiping her tears and smiling crookedly, "I don't drink. That's another thing we don't do as Muslims."

My eyes grew as she went on, "It leaves you intoxicated, pretty much able to do whatever you want without any consequences, which is why most people actually resort to it, so that they can be free of responsibilities for a while, no care in the world. Oh, and it gives you a pretty nasty head-ache."

As I looked at her through hazy eyes, I nodded, dreading the heaviness in them that was already beginning to take over, "Yeah, you're right. Big time. "

She laughed and then quickly halted, angling her head to look above the crowd, her eyes squinting, "Oh boy. I think Zack's spotted me. Better make a run for it. See you later, Katie."

She jumped off her seat and made her way towards the dance floor, squeezing herself into the crowd and blending in until I could no longer make her out.

I closed my eyes, as the music continued to pulsate around me, wondering if I should get up and leave. A slight pounding in my head had already begun and it was only a matter of time before my eyes would give way.

Hearing a familiar, loud laugh, my eyes shifted to the side where a less noisy bunch of people were dancing, and

I immediately noticed Sophie rocking her head to music, standing out in the black dress I'd last seen Demi Lovato wearing, the wheelchair doing no harm to the perfect moves she was performing as she whipped her hair around, ecstatic and energized by the music. Jayne moved by her side, laughing at the top of her lungs as she filmed Sophie on her video camera.

Sensing my stare, Jayne glanced my way and waved, then bent down to whisper in Sophie's ear, as she too looked up and grinned broadly. They both made their way over as a rap song started and then started comically wiggling their hips to it, their uncoordinated moves leaving me in hysterics.

"You guys should make your own music video. The general public has a right to witness such *unique dance moves,*" I snickered, as Sophie stuck her tongue out at me.

"But who would sing for us?" Jayne joked.

"I wouldn't mind," said a deep voice, coming from behind me. I whipped around to find Max Swift standing there, offering me a cocktail and smiling broadly at us.

"I've already had one too many," I said politely, feeling nauseous just by looking at it.

"Suit yourself," he said, swiftly placing it on a tray as a waiter passed by and then turning back to us. "You girls having a nice time?"

"The time of my life," I muttered, as Jayne stifled a laugh beside me.

"Well with looks like yours who wouldn't manage to have a

good time," he said, his eyes on me the entire time.

I groaned inwardly, and pointedly looked away as my eyes scanned the crowd.

"Looking for someone, Katie?"

"No...I...well...."

"Well then, how about a dance?" he stated, finishing off his drink and then grabbing my hand.

"Uh...no thanks," I immediately pulled my hand out of his.

"Why not?" he pouted.

"I'm exhausted, really I am, why don't you ask...err...Laura there?" I suggested, pointing at a besotted Laura standing to the side.

"Laura? Are you kidding me? And what happened to dancing the night away? You can't be serious," he said, raising his eyebrows at me.

"Dancing the night away is over-rated. Nobody ever actually does that."

"I thought you were the type who was up for a challenge. Why not set the new record?" he declared, pulling me by the hand again.

"I'm just really not in the mood, Max," I snapped, yanking my hand out of his.

104

"Oh, I get it, this isn't even about the dancing is it?" he asked, his voice taking on an icy tone.

"What are you talking about?"

"This is about you not wanting to ruin your reputation by hanging out with me. Well I've got news for you, Katie Anderson, any girl at this party, or better yet our entire school would snatch even the smallest chance at being with me. Now I'm gonna ask you one more time, will you dance with me?" His voice rising, his confidence growing as a crowd formed around us.

"I am not *any* girl. *This girl*, as a matter of fact, would snatch even the smallest chance to be *away* from you, and your obnoxious personality. So thank you Max, honestly for choosing me over the hordes of girls that surround you. And no thank you, *I do not want to dance with you.*" With that said I sat firmly on my seat again and glared at him, daring him to make more of a fool of himself. And surprisingly, he did.

"I see. Well, I guess that would just be expected from a goodie-two-shoes nun like you," he turned his attention to the crowd, "When was the last time Katie went out with anyone, huh? Is it just me or is the fact that she hasn't dated for the past year kind of shifty?"

"Leave her alone, Max. She doesn't have to answer to you. When was the last time you considered being single and taking your stuck-up attitude somewhere else?" Jayne growled at him, stepping in front of him in an effort to get him to leave.

He ignored her and instead rested his sardonic gaze on me, awaiting an answer.

My head began throbbing even more and I felt like I might faint any moment, but still held my ground.

"Max, you don't know anything about me or what I'm like. Don't judge me based on what you *think*, but on what you *know*, which is nothing. I think it would be best if you just left. I don't want to cause any problems. So just go."

He moved Jayne aside firmly and then stepped closer to me, eyeing me nastily. "No girl turns me down so what is it that really makes you different from everyone else? What is it O Silent Katie? Cat got your tongue now? What is it, *nun*?"

Suddenly out of nowhere a fist flew out and hit him straight in the jaw, and the next thing I knew Max Swift was sprawled on the floor, his lip bleeding and Jeff was standing over him.

Chapter Eleven

"Correct me if I'm wrong, but I believe Katie just told you to leave," Jeff declared, his fists clenched tightly by his sides.

Max furiously pushed himself off the floor and glared at Jeff. Wiping blood off his mouth, he said, "I wouldn't mess with me Collins. I can take care of myself pretty well."

"I don't doubt that, but then so can I. But unfortunately for me, I don't want a fight as much as you do so *back off*," Jeff replied, as a mass of bulky and loyal footballers arranged themselves around him.

"You heard him. *Leave Katie alone or deal with us!*" A bulky blonde defender yelled, placing himself right in front of Max and prodding him in the chest.

Max, who happened to be part of the school football team

himself, and had previously held quite a lot of respect for Jeff, stepped back in resignation. He shot me one last look of disgust before he sneered, "Fine, I'll leave her alone. I'm gonna go find myself some snacks to munch on and somebody who's more willing to dance. But next time this won't end so pretty."

"There won't be a next time," I heard myself say before whipping around and leaving the party, the music, and everything else I had started to hate about my life.

I ignored the whispers, the stares and the raised eyebrows, and instead looked ahead calmly as I made my way out. As I stepped outside into the cold night, I suddenly felt relieved, as if something inside of me had lifted, the pain in my head had lessened and I felt alive once again. The icy blast of air that hit me suddenly felt much better than the smothering heat inside, I lifted my face to the sky as my eyes rapidly filled with tears.

I scanned the stars and glorious full moon, wondering for a moment where this all came from, how we came to exist, and if there was really a God out there.

Oh God, if there is one and if you're out there. Help me, because I really need to sort out my life right now and I have no idea how to. Where to start and what to do, I need direction....I need.... I laughed through my tears as I realized just how strange this seemed, talking to God in my head. But....it felt good, it felt right. And so I continued, *I need guidance. A whole lot of guidance. And I need someone to listen to me, someone to talk to and confide in, and if I have to resort to imagining an invisible God, so be it. My life's already a big mess, so what harm could this be. If you're listening and if you're there, thank you.* I shook my head and laughed softly to myself again and then walked slowly to the bus stop just ahead. Who cares if I get seen near a bus stop? Shoot me.

"What are you laughing at?"

I didn't have to turn around to know who was talking to me.

"My life. If that's what it could be called. My *messed up* life," I said, sitting down on the bench and putting my head in my hands.

"I don't think your life's messed up. You've got quite a lot going for you. Don't you think?"

"I don't think you want to hear my answer to that," I replied bitterly.

There was silence. As if Jeff was really trying to figure out how to reply to me, but couldn't.

"I'm sorry."

"Excuse me?" I asked, lifting my head up at last.

"I'm sorry. I shouldn't have gone and punched Max like that, I just…I was so mad…I…I wasn't thinking straight and…"

I looked at him in bewilderment.

Jeff continued, just as flustered as before, "I mean, it wasn't right, all that he was saying, it was so…I…"

"Wait. Are you *apologizing*, Jeff?" I stared at him with wonder as he looked down, still uneasy. "No, no, it was…*definitely* the right thing to do. Granted, it was kind of violent," I smiled slightly then seeing him grimace once more, added in quickly, "I mean, at least it got him to leave me alone, right? Thanks."

He shuffled his feet, "It was nothing."

"You're being modest."

"It was the right thing to do and anyone would have done it."

"Is your hand alright? Did you break anything?"

His mouth twitched, "I know how to throw a punch, Kay."

"Oh."

We were silent for a moment as we thought about what to say next. It had felt strange suddenly falling back into our usual friendly banter after the confrontation at school earlier. As the silence grew, I knew that both our thoughts were on the earlier incident, and a feeling of uneasiness filled the air. I wanted him to apologize, to say that he hadn't meant any of the things he'd said before, to acknowledge that he had been rude and to tell me that he would be there for me. That although Islam had surged itself into my life without an announcement, changing everything I had ever known, it did not have to change me. It would not change me.

Finally, he spoke. "I don't believe we finished our conversation earlier."

Conversation? It had been more of a confrontation. From his reserved expression, it didn't seem like an apology was coming next, and immediately I felt my anger spark up again.

Matching his clipped tone, I retorted, "I believe it ended when I stormed off. Or was that not clear enough for you?"

He did a double-take. Looking away, he brushed back his hair in frustration and paced a few steps before returning his gaze to me, "You're still angry."

"You never apologized," I stated firmly, crossing my arms.

"I didn't think I had to," he spoke back slowly, in a measured tone. "I apologize if I came out too strong, but I don't take back any of my words."

Detesting being spoken to like a child, I narrowed my eyes and hissed, "Well, too bad, because they didn't change anything."

He opened his mouth to speak and then gritted his teeth, as if fighting back a retort. As calmly as he could manage, he said, "Look, Katie, this isn't about winning a debating competition or proving how strong-willed you can be. This is about making the right decisions and choices and all I'm trying to point out to you is that you need to give your dad a second chance. You need to give Islam a second chance. There's no sense in fighting it, you need to accept the change."

Anger rising, I looked him dead in the eye, "*And what if I won't?* What if I *want* to be nonsensical? What if I *want* to fight it?"

He looked at me for a long moment, anger drowning out of his eyes and replaced by pity, his shoulders relaxing and his body slacking slightly. For a sliver of a moment, he looked defeated. And then just as fleetingly, it was gone.

"Then you'll never feel at peace. With your dad, with your life, with your… future."

His words caught me and immediately I looked away, dropping

my gaze to the cobbled pavement. My heart thrumming loudly in my ears, I felt my hands tremble and my mind swirl. *Peace.* A feeling that I had already been fighting to hold on to. *How could he have known that?*

"There you guys are!" Jayne exclaimed suddenly, causing us both to jump slightly. "I was searching everywhere for my black jacket but couldn't find it. And then voila! I remembered I left it in Eva's room," she grinned and then suddenly picking up on the tension in the atmosphere, her smile faded. "Everything okay, guys?"

I didn't know how to respond and was glad when Jeff spoke, "Yeah, yeah, everything's….I was just umm… telling Katie that we'll give her a ride home."

My head snapped up to look at him, but he didn't meet my gaze. Hesitating momentarily, I said, "And I said that I… I'll get myself a ride." Even as I felt Jeff turn to glance towards me, I spoke quickly, "You guys live so close and you'd be going out of your way to drop me."

"Nonsense," Jayne waved a hand away.

"And…and I want to have some time to myself. Alone." I blurted out.

Even as I said this, I knew that it wasn't completely the truth; the real reason I was rejecting a ride home was that I needed someone to confide in, someone to hear about how awful my day had been, and someone to look me in the eyes and tell me that there was nothing to worry about. To tell me that the guilt that was tearing me apart wasn't because I had finally found a hole in my supposedly 'perfect' life but was because I was stressed out, to tell me that it was okay to occasionally be scared out of my mind, and to tell me that they would be there for me throughout it all. With Jeff in the car, this wasn't very likely.

Jayne looked at me and then Jeff and then back at me. "Oh, I see."

"How will you get home?" Jeff asked.

Now that's the part that I didn't have figured out. But somehow the next thing I knew I was dialling a number that I had learnt by heart and had used endlessly before, and holding my phone to my ear. I shifted myself around and ran my fingers through my hair nervously, waiting impatiently for someone to pick up, yet at the same time hoping that they wouldn't.

"Katie?" the voice on the other end asked hesitantly.

"Can you come get me?"

"Umm…yeah…yeah, sure. Where are you?"

"In Kensington, the third mansion on Campden Hill Road. You'll be able to spot it by the number of cars parked outside."

"Okay, then……I'll be there in ten."

"Wait! Don't go. I…," I sighed tiredly, squeezing my eyes shut, I quickly muttered under my breath, "I'm sorry, Dad."

"Oh Bugger. Katie if I'm going to come get you, I don't want to hear any of that," he jokingly commanded.

I couldn't help grinning at that, finally feeling like I could be myself again.

"No more apologies," he said again, this time more serious.

And knowing my dad, I knew that by that sentence he meant much more. No more lies, no more regret, no more feelings of betrayal, no more sleepless nights and swollen eyes, no more wishing that everything that had happened in the last two weeks could have been different, because everything was going to be okay.

Chapter Twelve

I woke up to the sound of a beautiful melody and my eyes slowly
fluttered open as I tried to figure out where it was coming from.
It was a song somewhat familiar to me, as if I'd heard it somehow
before, yet I knew without a doubt that I had never actually
listened to something like this before. The deep, strong rhythmic
tune filled me with respectful admiration and a longing to hear
more. I wanted to lose myself to the song, and although I did
not understand what was being uttered I knew that the words
had a profoundly powerful meaning behind them. I lay my
head further into my pillow and closed my eyes as the beautiful
recitation enveloped me. And then just as abruptly as it had begun,
it finished. Just like that. I yanked my sluggish eyes open and
strained my ears to see if I was mistaken, but I wasn't. Irritated,
I moved my hands around the bed in search of my alarm clock,
until my hand hit something hard. 4:00 AM. Amazed by what had
just happened, I rolled over into a more comfortable position and
decided to make sense of it all in the morning. Closing my eyes,
I succumbed myself to sleep once again and wondered if the sound
of the front door gently closing was just my imagination.

"Katie!" I heard someone cheer as I forced my groggy eyes open, only to see a blurry image of Mark leaning before me and excitedly waving his hands in front of my face.

"Leave me alone," I groaned, twisting my pillow over my ears and turning my head away.

"Nuh-uh. It's past ten and you're still in bed."

"And I intend to stay this way," I mumbled into my pillow.

"Katieeee, get u-up!" he sang, as he yanked open the curtains.

"Go 'way."

"I said," he suddenly yanked my quilt and pillow from me, "time to get up."

"Mark," I warned, as I shielded my eyes from the harsh sunlight, "Don't make me get up and whack you," I leaned forward, a clearly dishevelled mess, and glared at him, "Give me my stuff back."

He ignored me, "I knew you'd come around Katie. Just a

116

matter of time. But still, it's good to see that you're finally here. According to my estimation, you weren't supposed to show up until another three days."

"Mark I will….," I started, just as a large red cushion smashed into his chest, causing him to stumble backwards. My mouth dropped open as I realized the cushion I had been preparing to throw at him was still hidden behind my back.

"Markie, leave your sister alone," my dad said, grinning at me from the kitchen entrance as I burst into laughter.

"Dad, what was that for? *You're* the one who sent me to wake her up," he grumbled back, still in a somewhat happy mood. He shot me a grin and mouthed '*Watch your back*'.

"Well…," I yawned, stretching my arms out, "as much as I hate to say this. Mission accomplished."

I lazily stood up and made my way to the bathroom. Just as I got to the door, I turned around and chirped, "By the way, what's for breakfast?"

"Blueberry pancakes," Mark said cheerfully.

"What's the occasion?" I asked.

My dad flushed slightly as Mark replied, "What do you think?"

I wiggled my eyebrows and flashed him a smirk as I proceeded into the bathroom.

Moments after washing up, I found myself sitting on one of Dad's comfortable suede stools at the kitchen table and finishing off yet another plate of pancakes. Mark had just left for university and I watched as my Dad circled the marble island top, holding his phone to his ear. Last night he had called to let my mum know that I'd be staying the night with him, much to her surprise, and now he was trying to get me out of classes for the day. Just then, he shut the phone with a wide grin on his face and bounded towards the seat in front of me.

"I take it Mum said yes?" I chuckled.

"Of course. When have my charming persuasive skills ever let me down?"

"In my case, many times," I joked.

He raised his eyebrows slightly and looked away, coughing slightly to cover his laugh. "And that's what the pancakes are for."

I laughed loudly at that. "So I guess this is one of those times?"

"Definitely," he said matter-of-factly, crossing his hands behind his head and leaning back in his chair comfortably.

I nodded my head slowly and looked down at my empty plate, wondering if there was any way out of the situation at hand. I wrung my hands together and pushed my chair back, then leaned forward again and began to tap at the table until my dad gently laid his hand on top of mine and said, "Katie, want to go meet Big Ben?"

"What?" My head snapped back up.

"Grab your shoes and meet me at the front door." He stood up and pushed his chair back in, leaning on it slightly as he eyed my bewildered face. "I think we both need some fresh air."

We're walking down the street at a slow pace, hand in hand, as Dad points out monuments and bridges and anything and everything that has ever caught his eye in London. It had started with an early, sunny morning and my dad getting ready to go for his daily jog and me begging him to take me with him. And now, rather than me slowing him down, he was eagerly stopping here and there to point out his favourite places to me and re-living his childhood with every story that was recounted.

"Daddy, who's Ben?" I ask, interrupting him momentarily.

"Ben?" He asks back.

"Yeah, Big Ben," I say, tugging on his hand until he stops walking. "Mummy and Gran sometimes talk about him. Gran said the day Big Ben stops working is the day she'll remember to take her pills."

He bends down until he's my height, all the while trying to fight a smile. "Oh really? And what did mummy say to that?"

"She said a number of cen-chu-ries was too long a wait and that she'd rather just buy Gran memory pills. And then Gran said to her, 'Who said I'll remember to take those?'"

Dad laughs loudly at that and says, "That would be the day."

"So who is he then?" I ask again, scrunching up my brow and huffing like any other impatient five-year old.

"How about instead of telling you, I show you?" He asks with a familiar glint in his eye.

"I get to meet him?!" I shriek.

He chuckles and ruffles my hair, "Yes. Today is the day that you, Katie Anderson, will meet Big Ben. Anything else?"

I smile slyly at him, "Gran usually buys me ice cream at this time."

"And what time is that?"

"Let's get some and then ask Big Ben."

"You," he laughs as he hoists me up on his shoulders, "are one unique child."

That day I did meet Big Ben, and much to my dad's amusement began to choke on my chocolate chip ice cream when I first laid eyes on him. He, to be precise, was the largest four-faced chiming clock in the whole world. After that whenever we went for a stroll we'd ask each other "Want to go meet Big Ben?" and just like that, it stuck.

Lit by the sun, the sky was a beautiful shade of turquoise and the wind light and airy making the temperature outside just perfect. I adjusted my hair for the fourth time as I waited for my dad to begin speaking. I knew that unlike all the other walks we had taken before, discussing assignments for school, planning holidays together, recounting the weeks' events to each other, this one would be distinctly significant for the both of us.

120

"I don't even know exactly when it started," he wondered aloud, rubbing the back of his neck and furrowing his brow, "but it was during my stay in Morocco that I actually became aware of Islam. The people in my architectural unit weren't enough so we had some local architect lend us a hand, and he and his entire team were Muslims. And you know how I work, supervising everything and dropping by at times to make sure the work's going smoothly, well the times I did I noticed how attuned they were to the call to prayer and —"

"The call to what?" I interrupted.

"Prayer. In Islam, Muslims are obligated to pray five times a day among other things. We'll get to that, don't worry," he smiled, "So I noticed how, as soon as they heard the call to prayer, they would put *everything* down and leave to pray. The first time I actually thought they were taking a lunch break." He chuckled at the thought and then turned to me, "It was amazing to watch, to see them put their religion before everything else and to do it with such steadfastness. And then they'd return from praying with these satisfied looks on their faces, carrying on with their work just like before. I...I was astounded; from all the countries I'd worked in I'd never come across something like this."

I caught the astonishment in his voice and looked up. The look on his face said it all, he was *fascinated*.

"Well, two months went by and the project was near to completion, everyone got along really well and I became good friends with the local architect, Abdullah. I think it was around that time that he started to preach to me about Islam, I was adamant and stubborn though, and told him more than once that I was content with my life and wanted no change. Of course that didn't lessen my curiosity one bit, so I rallied him with questions

121

after questions to throw him off, to uncover cracks I was sure I'd find in his religion, but each answer instead made me more and more doubtful about *my* perfect life."

I was stunned. That was exactly how I had felt for the past few days. Doubtful. Unsure. Confused. I'd wondered to myself if it was normal to feel this way when I could have been 'having the time of my life'. *But could I really? Was this all life was about? Growing up, studying, partying, worrying about the future but never really knowing why? Living every day, but never really knowing why? Why all of this was happening? Why we were here in the first place? And why it was that we were always made to feel so cut off and caged, so 'different' in a society that pushed us to conform to their ways of thinking and living, to their fantasy of enjoying life to the fullest, when really nothing could ever be further from the truth, because life, life itself, would never be enjoyable without purpose, without meaning.* Hearing that my dad had felt the same way at some point in his life gave me an immediate sense of relief and hope. So it wasn't just me then.

By now we had reached Big Ben, and the long walk had felt nothing less than relaxing. My dad had paused his story to gaze up at it but instead of following his gaze, I looked at him, amazed at how much he had changed in the recent weeks. He had let his ash blonde hair grow until it was at an acceptable length, just enough for him to be able to run his hands through when he was frustrated, he had also quite surprisingly and for the first time left his stubble to grow into a short beard. The smile lines etched on his face seemed to look like they had grown even deeper if it was possible than the last time I had seen him, but it was the look in his eyes that caught me, instantly impressing me, humbling me, and entrancing me all in one. A new light shone in his startling blue eyes that I had never had the privilege to witness before, adding a glowing beauty to his newer, more radiant smile which now I noticed was directed at me.

"Interested to hear the rest?" he asked.

I would have loved to utter one of those classical movie speeches, the ones that normally end with a pompous 'So over my dead body' line, but I couldn't. I just wasn't able to, because deep inside of me something was pulling me back, and I knew that it wasn't mere curiosity. It was urging me to find out more, to listen to what more could be said and not to hold back because of pride or arrogance. So, breaking away from the intense look in my dad's eyes, I replied "Yes," knowing in that moment that something had shifted within me, and that I had just taken the first step to finding answers.

We began to walk back at a slow pace, as my dad continued, "It wasn't easy imagining or even comprehending that there might be cracks in the life that I had lead for so long. Big Cracks. And I was scared. Oh, Katie, I can't even tell you how scared I was, not only about the repercussions of embracing Islam like losing you or Mark or my easy life, but I…I was so frightened because everything around me, everything in me, my logic, my every thought…pointed towards Islam and I knew that if I denied it, then I would lose the only chance I had to feel at peace again," he closed his eyes as a gust of wind blew his hair back and inhaled deeply, "Peace is an amazing feeling, Katie."

I wish I knew, I thought to myself. The past few days had been anything but peaceful as my mind had been thrown into chaos, wondering, searching, and fighting for some peace of mind.

"But even then," he shook his head, "after all that, after getting tired of asking questions, I still needed one last push in the right direction. And by the grace of God, I got it only a few days later. I had gone for a stroll to the local marketplace with a few friends early in the morning and aside from us there was no one else there.

Most of them were looking for gifts to take home or traditional souvenirs for themselves, I was still thinking about the latest conversation I had had with Abdullah and about the religious crisis that I was in and had sort of wandered off a little ahead of the rest of the group. None of the stores really interested me until I came across a bookstore, it was medium-sized, not too large and not too small, but filled with racks and shelves of books. It wasn't decorated with wall-sized posters advertising different books or filled with smiling salespersons at each turn, but something of it still called you in."

"It drew you in? A bookstore."

"Yeah, I mean, aside from the cashier at the front desk, it was empty and…and secluded but there was just something about it. Maybe I just needed some space then, but whatever it was, I ended up entering it, walking around for a few minutes and fingering different books. It was after I had flipped through two or three books that I realized it was a Muslim Bookstore."

I raised my eyebrows. Now *that* was something.

"Immediately I was rooted to the spot and thought of just walking out and joining the others, not getting more interested in this religion than I already was. But then as I was turning around, my eyes caught sight of this beautiful wall hanging and I was so drawn to it," he paused to wink at me, "that I walked up to it and read it. And it wasn't like anything I'd ever read before."

My dad stopped there and stared ahead as if stuck in this memory.

"Then?" I asked, itching with curiosity.

"I left the marketplace immediately and went in search of Abdullah, and once I found him I asked him to show me the Quran, the Holy book that Muslims believe in and follow. I was pumped with this feeling of excitement and fear and when he asked me to wash up first, I hurriedly did. See, Muslims have to be in a state of cleanliness when they read the Quran. So then he sat me down and said, "You can open the Quran to wherever you like and begin reading." The Quran is written in Arabic but this one had the translation written on the side, so I did exactly what he said.

After that, I was a changed man. I can't even describe to you the feeling that I got when I read those words, the truth in them so profound, unlike anything I'd ever read before in my life, and when I finally uttered the Arabic words that would make me Muslim."

By now, his eyes weren't just shining with light but with tears as well. I stared at my dad in awe, I had never seen him so close to tears whilst telling a story, or at any other time. Thinking this was it, I nodded, before suddenly remembering that he'd left something out.

"So what exactly did that wall hanging say anyway?"

He looked down at me and smiled as he tried to come up with the right words, "It was something like a poem...but not really. More like the author's thoughts and feelings. And it really gripped me for a moment because it wasn't written elaborately with lengthy adjectives and metaphors here and there, but you could just tell that each and every word was coming from deep within the author. I didn't know if the author was a man or a woman because it was only signed with initials, but what I did know was that the author was *Muslim*."

I waited for a moment for my dad to continue and then asked impatiently, "Well, are you going to tell it to me or what?"

"You should know your dad well enough, Kay, to know that my memory is as good as a goldfish's," he winked at me. "Plus, even if I did remember, it's really something you have to see for yourself."

"Wait....so you're telling me you just took ten minutes to explain this *amazing* wall hanging and....and that's it. And now you expect me to go all the way to Morocco—"

"Did I mention I bought the wall hanging?" he grinned, as I sputtered to a stop. "Not the original, you know, because it was too dear to the owner, but a copy. I've hung it in my room. And just so you know, love, we're home," he chuckled.

Trying not to grit my teeth at his laughing, I marched my way to his front door and entered the security code, mine and Mark's birthdates, and then made my way to my room to get changed. After spending a few weekends at my dad's condo after the divorce, my dad had made sure me and Mark chose bedrooms for ourselves, and by now I had furnished my room and added a whole new wardrobe of clothes. So it wasn't really hard when my dad sprung one of his new ideas on me, of what we would do that weekend, mountain-climbing, paint-balling, laser tag, to quickly get myself ready.

Now, I hurriedly changed into flannel trousers and a comfy long shirt and then slipped out of my room, briskly walking towards his bedroom. My eyes scanned the walls until they finally rested on a long black and white wall hanging. Moving up closer, I realized that he was right, it was beautiful. Written in delicate, slanting cursive, it reminded me of the letters written in Shakespearean time with simple feathers and ink, but yet it had a modern touch to it with the edges of the hanging outlined in silver and grey paint. I stared up at it and began to read.

Chapter Thirteen

What I Would Have Done

I can weep till my eyes become red and swollen

I can scream till my voice becomes weak and hoarse

I can feel remorse and regret as they envelop me whole

But I cannot repent and I cannot try

Because my chances are gone

You may laugh at me when I say that I wish I could be in the place of the most sorry man on earth right now, if it meant I had time

You may laugh at me when I say that I would not hesitate in selling all of my prized belongings for a donation to charity, oh but I would hastily give them away, thrust them away from me, if it meant that they would not distract me

You may laugh at me when I say that I would willingly listen to those people who preached the faith that I heedlessly turned away from, those people who I scorned and rejected, if it meant that I would not be in this position right now

You may pity me for wanting to change it all

You may pity me for no longer having a say

You may pity me for wanting just one more day

But you do not feel this clinging, aching desperation that I do

You may mock me for saying that gossip circles
no longer entice me but isolation does

You may mock me for saying that money no longer attracts me
but reward does

You may mock me for saying that life no longer holds any
appeal for me but time does

You may be surprised to know that the most beautiful thing to
my eyes now is the picture of a humble servant in prostration to
God

You may be surprised to know that the most beautiful thing to
my ears now is the call to prayer, the words of God

You may be surprised to know that the most beautiful object to
me now is the Quran, the book of God

Yet the beauty that God graced humanity with, no longer holds any appeal for me for vanity also cost me time

You may be humbled in knowing that I would give the world, I would gladly give my soul, I would give anything just to meet my Creator

And finally, dear friend, I must inform you of one more thing...

I still hold on to the minute hope that one day, after years of pain and suffering beyond imagination, I will.

For surely a God so Merciful will reward me for the times that I closed my eyes and went forth with a decision trusting only Him,

For the times that I lay in bed at the peak of midnight, whispering prayers to Him,

For the times that I hid my sins from others and did not boast of my good actions to others,

For the times that I taught my children and my grandchildren how to pray even when I did not,

For the times that I visited my parents in the hospital, crying at their beds, holding their hands and allowing them to smile some more,

For the times that I broke down and repented to God when I felt like my life was too out of control.

You may think all of the harsh and spiteful things that you want of me but let me leave you with some advice

What I did, you may be doing right now
And that means that you and I are the same

But for one aspect, one significant aspect

My time is up but yours is still running

My time is up but yours is still running. The words echoed in my head over and over again. My eyes grew wide as I fumbled around in my head for an excuse to not feel this way, *so guilty.* Time. I rubbed my fingers on my throbbing forehead and tried to calm down. Was it? Was I running out of time? And what was that last thing about pain and suffering? *If it were true then how come no one had warned me about this before? Was I too late?*

"It's terrifying isn't it?"

I gasped and spun around. "Dad! *Don't do that to me!*"

"Do what?"

I narrowed my eyes and placed a hand on my hip. "Creep up on me like that. I swear it's like *you want me to get a heart attack.*"

"Don't be silly. Here, I brought you some hot chocolate."

I took the mug from him and smiled slightly. "Just the way I like it?"

"Three tablespoons of chocolate powder, heated to the point that it nearly burns off your dear fathers fingers, and served with marshmallows, white not pink."

"You have learned well." My smile grew a little, but I couldn't manage to laugh, not with what was going on in my head. I sat down on a beanbag, crossed my legs and slowly sipped the hot chocolate, my eyes on the view of the faraway roads below.

"So, what do you think?" I could feel his stare from where he stood, leaning beside the hanging.

"It is."

"Is what?"

"Terrifying." I looked up at him now, "I don't understand some of it, the pain and suffering part mostly. And....why the person seems so *desperate*," I whispered the last part.

"Are you ready to listen?" he asked softly.

I nodded.

"Questions?"

"Plenty."

"Then let's get started."

"I've got too many questions in my head. I don't know where to start," I exclaimed helplessly, as my dad and I sat on the living room couches.

"Okay, then let me start." After a moment, he asked, "How do you think we were created? I mean, where do you think this all came from?" he gestured around with his hands.

I furrowed my brow, "I definitely don't believe in evolution or any theories like that. Mum taught me that God created us, and I always just went along with that but...recently I've been thinking about it for myself and it just seems right. Like something is behind all of this, like a....God. But that's where it stops. I don't think beyond that."

He nodded his head, "And do you believe that Jesus is God or the son of God? Or both?"

My eyebrows rose in surprise as I suddenly realized that I'd never asked myself that, never given it a moment's thought and had just accepted it. Staring ahead now, I mulled it over in my head for a few moments and then responded carefully, "No. No, I don't believe that Jesus is God. I know it sounds silly but I just can't....he's *human...* and God...God can't be human. It's just impossible. And Jesus was crucified but God can't *die*, that's not…"

"Not what?"

I looked at him, "Logical. I probably sound crazy..." I shook my head.

"No, no, go on," he urged.

I twisted my hands together, "I don't know what Muslims believe but I…my mind just can't accept that. It would be like accepting that the creator died, but then, *who's running everything*? It doesn't sound rational. God can't be *human* or," I pondered for a moment, "anything else created because –"

"The Creator cannot be created."

I blinked, "Exactly. It wouldn't make sense at all. Especially since in Christianity we're told to follow Jesus, but he also prayed to God, so then why would a 'God' *pray* to another God and tell us to do the same? It's just too confusing."

"So if you don't believe he's God, then do you still believe he's the son of God?"

"No," I shook my head vehemently.

"Why not?"

"Because…because," I started, floundering as I tried to put my feelings into words.

He leaned forward, "The claim that Jesus is His son means that God can have children and that means that He's not unique or different from His creation. And the Creator cannot be similar to the creation. God is unique and transcendental."

I stared at him with bug-eyes, completely at a loss with words, affirming what he'd just stated. *How had he just read my mind?*

He smiled knowingly, as if he knew exactly what I was thinking then, "Katie Anderson, you're closer to being Muslim than you are to being Christian. Everything you just said is part of our belief as Muslims, and completely contradictory to Christian beliefs."

"You're joking," I swallowed.

"No, I'm not. One of the chapters in the Quran actually states, '*Qul huwa Allah hu ahad*' – Say He is God, the One and Only, '*Allah hus-Samad*' - God is Eternal and Absolute, '*Lam yalid wa lam yulad*' - He neither begets nor is He begotten, '*Wa lam yakun lahu kufuwan ahad'* - And there is none comparable unto Him," he said, ticking off each point on his fingers. "And that is one of the most essential parts of our belief, in fact it's the *foundation*. To acknowledge God, know His attributes and believe in Him, and as a result, *worship Him*. It makes up the first part of the Islamic testament - *There is none worthy of worship except for God.*"

I was silent, absorbing it all with a shocking sense of calm, even as my mind buzzed with a tingling excitement. What my dad had just done was beyond me, but in some wondrous way, he had managed to cross through the web of confusing thoughts in my mind, to halt the incessant questions niggling at me, and to give me a sense of peace at last. Overwhelmed with mixed emotions, I realized then that he had given me answers.

Chapter Fourteen

An hour later, I sat at the kitchen counter with my head propped in my hands as my eyes followed my dad's movements. Shortly before, he had excused himself from our discussion to go and pray the afternoon, obligatory '*Dhuhr*' prayer in the Mosque, whilst I set about making lunch. He had returned just as I began to set the table and politely asked if I wouldn't mind waiting for him as he prayed his voluntary prayer. I had of course agreed and eagerly taken a seat at the kitchen counter, an excellent vantage point from which I could inconspicuously watch him pray in his bedroom.

From the very moment he raised his hands in surrender to begin praying, I was engrossed; eyeing his every move. Watching someone pray was unlike anything I'd ever done in my entire life, it was like a window into their soul, and even as I knew this was something personal, being performed in the solitude of an empty room, I couldn't tear my eyes away.

I'd kept my distance from the Church as long as I could remember, never wanting to devote myself to the religion, and the only other time I'd seen someone pray had been at the hospital when I was nine and Mark had been admitted for surgery for his appendix.

As I sat in the waiting room, I recall openly staring at the over-emotional woman in the seat next to mine, as she cupped her hands together, bowed her head slightly, and cried, "*Please. Please, God, help him. Just like Jesus. Just like Jesus. Who died and suffered for us. Give Jason the strength to withstand suffering the way Jesus did, to bear it in union with him, to offer it with him to atone for his sins. O Jesus, make my Jason strong so he can work for your honour and glory and the salvation of all people. O Mary, helper of the sick, pray for my Jason. Make him better…*" It wasn't until my mum pinched me, that I looked away, and even then I continued to listen, my nine-year-old mind registering confusion at her desperate plea to three different sources, and embarrassment at her obliviousness.

Now, though, as I watched my dad prostrate humbly to the ground, I felt nothing but respect and reverence for him. He believed and worshipped only one God, every call and plea directed solely towards Him. Wasn't that what I had wanted, what I was searching for? *Then what was holding me back?* I recalled a part of the discussion we had earlier that had stunned me no less than the concept of the oneness of God in Islam, as I sat pensively thinking.

"*So who was Jesus then?*" *my dad asked.*

"*Not the son of God.*"

"*Not the son of God,*" *he reiterated with a smile.*

"*He was,*" *I spoke slowly, as I thought it over,* "*a devout believer in God. Who called to the worship of God.*"

"*So he was a Prophet of God?*"

"Well, I don't want to put a label on him..." I said, as I tried to remember exactly what a 'Prophet' entailed.

"In Islam, a Prophet is exactly that though. A devout believer in God who calls to the Oneness of God and His worship and is sent by God to guide humanity. To us, Jesus is not the son of God but the Prophet and Messenger of God," he explained.

I nodded, my eyes widening, "Yeah, that's what I believe."

"And unlike the Christian concept of salvation, Muslims actually believe that Jesus wasn't crucified or killed to atone for their sins."

"They don't believe in salvation?" I furrowed my brow, recalling the same declaration from Kitty not too long ago.

"Not in that way. In Islam, salvation is more like repentance and asking for forgiveness for ourselves. When we sin, we either pay the price for it, or repent for it. As for Jesus, we believe that he was saved by God, raised up to the Heavens where he will stay until God decrees that he return."

"But how do you know that? Where are you getting all this information from?"

"The Quran – the Holy Book revealed to us by God. It has the answers to all of your questions. Each Prophet and his story and the details of the Hereafter have been told in the Quran. It's the only book that has never been changed or altered over the years, sent down to the Prophet Muhammad and a guide for all of mankind, inviting them to Islam, detailing different aspects about Islam, from the lives of the Prophets to the jewels and blessings in Heaven, and from the signs of the Day of Judgement to the severe punishment of the Hell Fire. All of what I just told you comes directly from the Quran and that's not *all, there is information in the Quran that no illiterate shepherd could have known more than 1400 years ago, information that scientists discovered just recently, in the nineteenth century. There are numerous miracles proving the divinity of the Book."*

Thinking back now, I realized that there was no use questioning what he had said, no use of ignoring the challenge that he had set for me, to read the Quran and discover the truth for myself.

"Mmmm, that was good," my dad said, as I pushed back my seat and walked over to the kitchen sink.

"You'd think there might have been some left-overs after cooking a meal for five, but not when you're around," I laughed, as I watched him goofily lick his plate clean.

"Only when you're cooking," he winked at me, getting up to clear the rest of the table, before walking over to me with a grin spread across his face, "I had a good time today."

"Me too," I nodded, dunking the plates into the sink.

"So what did you think about the uh…," he cleared his throat consciously, "you know, stuff we talked about…," he coughed, "prior to now."

An amused smiled tugged at my lips as I asked slowly, "The discussion we had earlier?"

"Yeah," he breathed out.

"It was…," I searched for words to describe it, "far from bromide."

"Huh?"

I laughed, "I loved it, Dad. It was great. And um thanks," I glanced at him meaningfully, "You cleared up a lot of questions I had. Stuff I'd never thought about and that really mattered to me," I finished, averting my gaze quickly.

"Katie," he waited for me to look up at him and then said softly, "I know this is a lot to take in. I know how you feel, *how you've felt*. It was the same with me. And from the day you were born I've known your heart," he lay a hand on my cheek as my eyes welled up with tears, and he continued, "Your sincere and compassionate heart. Be truthful to yourself and just this once follow your heart. Free your soul."

"I'm trying, Dad," I choked out, and then realized that I was crying.

In the next moment, he was pulling me into his arms and rubbing my back gently, whispering soothing words to me until finally my eyes had dried. I couldn't remember the last time I had cried with my head on my dad's shoulder, but it felt familiar and right. What he had said shook me because it was all so genuinely coming from his heart. And he was right, he did know how I felt and how I was feeling right now, otherwise how else was he to know that what I wanted most right now was to *be free*.

"I guess this means a trip to Debenhams," he said after a good couple of minutes, interrupting my thoughts.

I looked at him questioningly and then at the finger pointing at his damp shirt. I opened my mouth to laugh only to find myself acutely embarrassed when a strangled hiccup escaped in its place.

"Err...sorry about the shirt," I hastily said, my face flushed, as I moved out of his embrace. There was no reply as my dad broke into a fit of laughter, and then seeing me adjust my hair nervously, cracked up a lot more.

"What," I snapped, "is so funny?"

"You're...doing...the hair...thing...again," he managed to get out before starting all over again, and then quickly held up a finger before I could snap at him again and said, "But I have to say it is better than what Mark does when he's nervous."

I covered my face and shook my head, trying not to let him see the grin on my face.

"That," he went on, his voice entirely too amused, "blinking thing he does with his eyes. A blink a second, I call it."

"Stop, Stop!" I exclaimed, holding out my hand and laughing. "Just wait till I find out you're nervous secret."

"If there is one," he grinned and then looked down at his watch and let out a low whistle, "Wow, can you believe it's three already?"

I realized then that he had been trying to distract me from crying my heart out and it had worked. What dad wanted to watch his teenage daughter turn into a helpless puddle? I smiled slightly, "I think mum's expecting me home soon."

"Yeah, come on, I'll drive you there. If you have any more err...

questions, you can ask on the way," he picked up his car keys and headed for the front door, beckoning me to follow.

I trailed after him, my eyes involuntarily staring at the wall hanging again, as my steps slowed in front of his room. It had been signed *SB,* and I wished just for a moment that I knew who had written it, who was responsible for catching my dad's attention and leading him to Islam, because if I could meet them right now I would want to say only one thing. *Thank You.*

My dad was a changed man. And I had a feeling that he wasn't going to be the only one that would follow their heart.

"Katie," he hollered now, "are you coming or what?"

I stared at it for another second, before yanking my gaze away and hurrying after my dad, following him was one habit that I hoped to never break.

Chapter Fifteen

"Miss Anderson, care to share with the class what is so vividly capturing your attention outside that window?" Mr Stevens, my English teacher and by far my favourite, asked in an amused tone.

I yanked my head up to find that I had caught not only his attention but the entire classroom's as well. It was probably one of the first times that I was being stared at for something other than my beauty and popularity. Wrenching my gaze away from the onlookers, I swallowed and desperately looked outside to see if maybe miraculously something amazing, like a visit from Prince William, were taking place, after all it wasn't like it hadn't happened before.

"In a city like London, I'm shocked to find that rain still amazes some of us even now," he went on, hands behind his back and now trying very hard to fight off the smile that was growing on his face. For a forty-something married man with kids, and an impressive fourteen years of teaching at the same school, I still found it hard to believe how easily he could engage the classroom in laughter, as was happening right now. But then again, he is Irish.

"Sorry, Mr Stevens. I...had a lot on my mind," I said, my face flushed with colour.

"Clearly," he replied, but then shot me a reassuring smile before turning back towards the whiteboard.

More than a week had passed since my dad had introduced Islam to me, and I found it hard concentrating in class as thoughts swam around in my head. On the car ride home, I had questioned my dad as much as I could, he had explained what the call to prayer was, how Muslims prayed, and how if someone accepted Islam all they're past sins would be forgiven, and they would be as pure as a new born baby. I absorbed it all with an understanding that I never knew I had inside me, listening to him keenly, knowing that every time he spoke of Islam, my mind cleared and I felt lighter.

Finally when we had reached home I asked him what had held him back from accepting Islam. His reply, *'I was too scared of facing my imperfect life',* had made me begin to examine mine. I started hesitating before doing even the simplest things, asking myself if it was morally correct or not, and then why I even cared. Because I did, no doubt about it. All of it had not gone unnoticed by my mum, who demanded to know what my dad and I had talked about, and what we were discussing on the phone every day. Not ready to open up yet, I had left her tight-lipped at home once more, as I scrambled through my jumbled thoughts.

"What's wrong?" Jayne whispered, suddenly bringing me back to the present as she came into my view, leaning to speak to me from her seat in front of mine.

"I'll tell you about it later," I whispered back.

She was leaning close enough for me to be able to see the genuine concern that flickered in her warm, tawny eyes as she watched me closely. With a small nod, she turned back, allowing me to stare blankly ahead once more. Just then the bell rang, snatching me away from my thoughts and leaving me very confused as I watched my classmates jump out of their seats whilst some had already reached the door. I felt a tap on my shoulder and looked up to see Jayne standing there, waiting patiently, her bag slung over her shoulder.

"What class do we have now?" I asked, hurriedly putting my books away and standing up. I threw my bag over my shoulder and turned around to see Jayne staring at me with an odd expression on her face.

"What?"

"Classes are over dummy. What planet are you on?" she half-teased, a lace of concern in her voice.

"I...I...forgot to check the time," I answered slowly, confusion clear in mine.

"O-kay," she raised her eyebrows, "there's definitely more to this. How was your weekend at your dad's?"

I looked at her with a startled expression, "Oh, it was…good. You know, the usual," I mumbled, taking a step towards the door.

"And how was your talk about Islam?"

I froze, "How—"

"What?" she placed a hand on her hip, "You think I wouldn't

be able to deduce that by myself? It's pretty obvious, Kay. You're not here anymore."

I turned to her, "What do you mean?"

"You know, you're in your own world," she gestured around with her hands vaguely, "You're lost."

"I'm not lost, I'm—"

"Searching, I know. And I'm happy for you. Finally," she smiled slightly, "It's about time you started. I was wondering when you were going to…"

"Wait? You *knew*?"

"Kay, this is me you're talking to. *Jayne*. Master of espionage."

I chuckled, "Yeah, right. Really, how could you tell?"

"Fine, it was at the dance," she confessed begrudgingly. I looked at her in confusion so she continued, "You weren't dancing. That kind of gave off a lot of signals. You looked utterly bored at a party you'd spent three hours getting ready for, and that last line you threw at Max, *whoa*," she nodded indignantly, "now *that* was some serious stuff. *'There won't be a next time.'*" she mimicked me.

I was quiet, realizing now that she was right, I had been pretty obvious. *What was I thinking?*

"It's all right, Kay. No one suspects a thing," she laid a hand on my arm, "Lily Barnes vomiting all over Max kind of took all the spotlight off of you. Only I could still tell. I told you," she pointed at herself proudly, "master of—"

"Espionage," I grinned, "Agreed."

Her phone suddenly rang then. Picking it up, she looked at the caller ID and her face registered confusion. She answered it and then slowly a smile spread across her face, she nodded enthusiastically as she replied to the caller and then ended the phone call.

She turned to me and beamed, "Well, that was Mum."

Grabbing my hand, she headed towards the classroom door, pulling me along. "She was asking if we'd like to go get a bite to eat with her right now. She just finished designing the Szalinski's house, so she's in the mood of celebrating."

"Sounds great," I smiled, "You go ahead. I'll catch up with her another time."

"Sure?" she asked, slowing her footsteps as she turned to me, remembering suddenly how abruptly our conversation had ended.

"Positive," I laid my hands on her shoulders as I spoke with assurance, "We can talk all about me and my 'search'," I connoted with my fingers, "later. I know you've been dying for some quality time with your mum. Plus, I'm a bit drained myself, so I think I'll head home."

"All right, shall I tell Jeff to give you a ride? He's been asking about you lately," she said, fetching her phone out of her pocket again.

As we stepped out into the sunlight, I stopped her, "No, don't call him. It's okay, Mark's picking me up, as usual. His university is only a couple of minutes away."

"Kay," her voice softened, "you and Jeff have to work things out. It's been days since you've spoken to each other."

"I know," I said, realizing just then how much I was beginning to miss him. We'd never gone this long without speaking to each other, and it felt odd, seeing him around the school grounds and yet not speaking to him. Even as I began to delve more into learning about Islam, I acknowledged to myself that Jeff had been right, but somehow I couldn't find the courage to admit that to him. Or that I was beginning to see a new side to Islam. I needed more time, time to digest everything about Islam, before I took steps to fixing my life.

"It's...it's the whole Islam thing," I finally said, "I mean...I don't know what I think about it yet...but...I...I don't feel comfortable in the car...," I struggled to come up with the right words while at the same time watching her expression change every few words from concern to surprise to utter bewilderment, "—I mean....what I'm *trying* to say is...I *do* feel comfortable in the car because it's a very....umm *comfortable* car...but not in the presence of Jeff," I finished quickly.

Her jaw dropped open as her wide eyes continued to stare at me, and then we both launched quickly into another conversation of sputtering and floundering.

"Oh. This is about that day right? When Jeff accused you of being ashamed and embarrassed. *Right? Oh my god, I should have known!* No wonder you've been acting so weird around him lately! You haven't even ridden in the car with us these past few days. Man, Kay, why didn't you tell me? I would have —"

"What I meant to say was....not in the presence of...of umm...a man. Guy. Man. I...it's not me. I'm not against guys or anything

150

but...it just feels awkward because I'm thinking about Islam right now and if I were to think that way—"

"—made him beg you for, like, forgiveness. He was totally out of line. Didn't I say that before? And you were like, 'No Jayne, maybe he's right'. *Come on!* I can clearly see how unaffected you are by what he said —"

"—then I wouldn't want to spend time with a guy....man... member of the opposite sex…freely and you know hang out and all because...because...that's not allowed in Islam. You see, that's all it is. As soon as I'm certain about what I'm going to do next I'll... *wait, what are you saying?"*

"—because you've hardly been listening to a word I've been saying," she ended triumphantly, and then furrowed her brow as if remembering something suddenly. "Wait, did you say something about Islam?"

"Oh my God. That's all I was talking about right now. Didn't you hear a word I said?" I slapped my forehead in exaggeration.

"Well, finally you're on the receiving end of having to talk endlessly and not be heard," she replied, her mouth twitching as she tried unsuccessfully to fight back a smile.

I groaned. "*You* were talking about that Jeff incident that happened a week ago and by which I am *not affected* and *I* was talking about not being in the presence of a *man* until I get all my emotions and thoughts sorted out, and make a decision."

I spoke to her so meaningfully that even I nearly believed it. In truth, I had begun to realize that Jeff might mean something to me, that after years of being his best friend I might just want something else, and that after watching him come to my rescue the night of the party, something had changed. I suppose absence really does make the heart grow fonder.

But my thoughts of Islam conflicted with that, and I knew that at this point in my life, it mattered to me more. I needed to find myself and bring peace to my heart before anything else. So, I pushed all thoughts of Jeff to the back of my mind, and caught on to anything that might help me avoid him, even if it meant passing on an opportunity to ride in one of my favourite Mercedes.

"Jeff's a man?" Jayne inquired.

"No, of course not, I meant guy."

"Right. So what do I tell Jeff?"

"How was your day?" Mark asked, one hand on the back of my seat, his body turned at an angle as he carefully manoeuvred his black BMW out of the car park.

"Don't ask," I replied back tiredly, my eyes shut and the cool air of the air-conditioner relaxing my nerves.

He laughed, "That bad? And here I thought Queen Bee's never had bad days."

I ignored his teasing and opened my eyes to focus my attention outside. The car park was swamped with all sorts of fashionable cars, but even then my eyes automatically centred in on Jeff and Jayne who were talking to one another just a few cars down. Now I could see that maybe it hadn't been all that wise of me to tell Jayne to 'improvise', seeing as Jeff looked as confused as ever.

"What are you doing with Dad this weekend?"

I blinked, suddenly remembering that we were supposed to spend the weekend together. "I haven't thought about it yet."

"You mean you forgot."

I smiled sheepishly at him, "That too."

He raised an eyebrow, reminding us both that this was a first.

"You look like you've got a lot on your mind. That coupled with the fact that on any other day you'd be more than willing to ride with the Collins leads me to believe that there is something definitely wrong with you."

"Really, Sherlock?" I asked drily.

"Or it may just be that you wanted to spend more time with me. You miss me, don't you?" he winked.

"As if," I rolled my eyes, with a small smile.

"Come on, Kay. You know you wanna tell me. What's bugging

you? What's on your mind?"

I sighed and slumped even lower in my seat. "Nothing."

"You're incredibly persuasive, you know," he half-smiled, turning towards me, "Aww, come on. It's me, Mark. You tell me everything," he egged on.

I fought back a smile, recalling that the last secret I'd ever entrusted him with had been when I was five. I snatched a glimpse at him, taking in his cheerfully wide smile, and realized that I hadn't many options; the car had just slowed to a stop amid the busy traffic jam around us, and simply the thought of Mark whining for the rest of the wait sent shivers down my back. On top of all that, I had to admit to myself that I was in great need of a listener at that moment. Even if it was Mark. I groaned inwardly, I had better not regret this later.

"It's Islam. I've just been thinking more about it lately, about," I hesitated, "maybe accepting it."

"Whoa," he breathed, as I warily remained still, not daring to look at him. "I did *not* expect that."

"Neither did I," I whispered, "but it just sort of...enveloped me or something. I can't stop thinking about it," I said with a hint of exasperation.

"Like, it's taken over your mind or something?" he sounded awe-struck.

I rolled my eyes at him, "No, but, maybe my conscience. It just, it seems like the right thing to do."

Mark stared at me with new eyes, "Wow, how much time did you spend with Dad? I mean, sure he cleared up all the misconceptions *I* had about Islam, but you...you're *converting?*"

"No, I'm not," I said quickly, "I mean, I'm *thinking* about it. I haven't made up my mind, it's just a thought." After a moment, I added in, "And even if I was hypothetically seriously considering it, there's nothing wrong with that," I shot him a look, "Islam's not a terrorist religion."

"I never said it was," he spoke slowly, "but *you,*" he pointed a finger at me, "have never been a religious person, so I'm just voicing my surprise here. I mean, where is this all coming from?"

I shook my head, "I don't know. I....what's the purpose of life, Mark?" I suddenly asked.

He was quick to answer, "Enjoyment. Fun. Parties."

"And then what?"

"Then we die. End of story. Nothing special."

"You really think that?" I asked quietly.

He looked away uncomfortably, "Well, yeah. From my experience, everything good always comes to an end. And...and what about you? How do *you* know Islam is the real deal? I mean, come on, sell it to me," he turned to me with a flourish, challenge in his eyes.

"I...I...," I flustered, and then suddenly felt angry, "How can you ask me that?"

He dropped his gaze as I continued, "Two minutes ago we were talking about my inability to even fully accept the thought of it, and now, now you wanna *prove* something? I don't need this from you."

He let out a sigh, "I'm sorry, Kay. I was out of line. I…I was just trying to look out for you. I guess I got a bit protective."

Right. Nice cover up. It was obvious to me that Mark hadn't closed the subject on religion yet either, even if he pretended to be oblivious to it.

The car began to move forward slowly and for several minutes, all was quiet. Mark cleared his throat consciously, breaking the suffocating silence, and asked hesitatingly, "So, why *are* you interested in Islam?"

Silently, I looked outside my window, gathering my thoughts carefully before saying, "It's clarified all these questions for me, these doubts I had before, and from what Dad explained about it, it's logical. It makes so much sense to me. Everything he's talked about up till now is…*right*. And he's been so helpful and I can see that he's trying really hard but….it…it's not something I can be convinced of overnight."

After a moment of pondering, Mark asked, "Why not?"

I turned to him incredulously, "*What?*"

"Hey," he said neutrally, "All I'm saying is that if you think it's right then why not just accept it?"

"Because this isn't something I can decide just like that!" I exclaimed in frustration, "This is my *life*. And I'm not denying it,

I am still thinking about Islam, *all the time*. I've been spacing out in class and…and at breakfast or dinner just because I'm thinking about this," I heaved a sigh, "and don't for a second think that Mum hasn't noticed. She's such a huge part of my life and I can't even talk to her about this."

"It's all right, I get it. I should be more understanding about this; I didn't know you were thinking about this so much," he glanced at me, "Again, I forget that you're no ordinary teenage girl who thinks about—" he made a face, "—shopping and boys all the time, but the fact that you're actually considering this shows me how mature you are."

"Mature? Was that supposed to be a compliment?" my mouth twitched.

"Kinda," he shrugged, with a grin.

"Well, what about *Mum* —" I started, remembering the look she'd given me before I'd left for school in the morning. A look that said '*I can't believe you*'.

"Mum always listens. Always. Even when she doesn't want to. And she's dealt with something…like this before so believe me, she cares."

I looked at him then, at his calm and passive face betraying none of his feelings. The car had also stopped. So I turned my head and noticed with surprise that we had reached home. It was frustrating knowing how easily I was being surprised these days when on any other day I was the one in control.

"Talk to her. I'm sure that all she's worried about right now is how you've been acting strangely for the past few days. She needs to know that you're all right," he went on.

"Wow, when did you become so…," I searched for the right word.

"Awesome?"

"Brotherly."

"Puh-lease," he feigned disgust as I grinned, "I'm just telling you what you need to hear."

I nodded my head as I unbuckled my seatbelt, holding his gaze for a moment longer, knowing that something had happened during this car ride that had shifted the entire dynamic of our relationship.

"Are you coming in?"

"No, I've got to get back to my dorm. I have some stuff to take care of. Plus, Mum's gonna be home soon and you two need to talk. Alone."

"Okay." As I turned to step out of the car, he said softly, "Katie, wait."

I looked back at him, "Hmm?"

He focused his gaze on his hands, "Whatever happens, I just want you to know that I'm fully supportive of whatever choice you make. I…I'll stand by you," he raised his head, "And I know that you will make the right decision, Kay. Don't get too worked up about it. You," he hesitated, "you've got amazing written all over you."

My eyes almost filling with tears, I spoke sincerely, "Thanks. That means a lot." I smiled slightly, "Coming from you."

"Hey, I wasn't that bad before!" he grinned, playfully punching me. "Well, take it from me. When the time comes to make a choice, you'll know what to do, and you might even submit."

I froze, staring at him in shock. *Submit.* One word, spoken so casually by my laid-back brother, was somehow instigating a mixture of feelings within me. My dad's voice replayed again and again in my head, "*Free your soul*," as Mark waved a hand in front of my face, his concerned face a mere blur in my vision. *Submit.*

"Katie, what happened? Did I say something?" his hands suddenly grabbed me by the shoulders, shaking me slightly.

Jolted back to the present, I shook my head to clear it and looked up at Mark, "Uh…no, no, I was just…thinking about something. It was nothing."

It was definitely not nothing. To anyone else, it might have seemed insignificant, but to me, right then, that moment meant something. Islam literally meant submission, and I couldn't deny that something within me was beginning to change.

Chapter Sixteen

Entering my house, I propped my bag on the floor, and plucked an apple from the fruit bowl on the kitchen counter before making my way to the living room. I sat down on the sofa, tucking my legs under me, and bit into it, all the while thinking of how exactly to approach the subject of Islam with my mum. Should I ask her about her views first? Should I mention how her lack of interest in religion is why I'm so confused myself? Or should I just plunge in and let her know that I'm interested in Islam? Would she even care? I mulled over each situation in my head, becoming more anxious by the minute until I had finally finished eating. Realizing then just how tired I was, I spread my legs out and pushed my head lower into the cushion, my eyes slowly fluttering shut. Perhaps, it was best to stop over-thinking the situation and let it unravel naturally. And with that last thought, I drifted off to sleep.

Someone was nudging me, my arm to be exact, and it wasn't at all entertaining. I shoved their hand away, and turned onto my side. And then somehow, the cushion underneath my head was being yanked out from under. Seriously, there should be a law against waking people up like that. I opened my eyes, preparing to give whoever that hand belonged to a piece of my mind.

My eyes narrowed, "Mum — "

"Finally! I've been trying to wake you up for the past ten minutes."

"*Why?*"

"*Excuse me*, but last time I checked you abhor sleeping during the daytime, you say it ruins your timing," she looked down at me, her hands on her hips.

"I wasn't sleeping, Mum," I moaned, closing my eyes sleepily, "I was just taking a tiny nap."

"Tiny? It's six o'clock."

My eyes sprang open, "Aww man. Why didn't you..." I started, and then shut up as she glared at me.

"*For the past ten minutes.*"

"Okay, okay, I'm up now."

"If you're hungry then there's some pasta in the kitchen," she added.

"Really? I'm starving," I rubbed my eyes, blinking a couple of times as I fully woke up.

"Okay, then I'll just pop some in the microwave for you."

"No mum, it's okay. I'll do it," I swung my legs off the couch, wondering why she was being this nice.

She was already making her way to the kitchen though and waved my remark away, "It's fine. We can talk while you eat. You might wanna wash up though; it looks like your eyes are fighting to stay open."

Ah, so that was the reason for her sudden mood change. *She wants to talk.* "Yeah, I had no idea I was this exhausted."

"When you've got a lot on your mind that's bound to happen."

I raised my eyebrows, was I really that readable? "I'll just be a minute," I mumbled with a yawn, as I made my way to the bathroom.

I sauntered into the kitchen few minutes later, sniffing the air, "Mmm that smells really good."

"I picked it up from the new Italian restaurant that opened up down the street."

I looked up at her, "I thought that place took months just to book. How did you —"

"Sam."

I grinned, "That explains it."

Sam, an assistant of my mum's, and the daughter of one of the best Italian chefs in London, had a certain knack for always getting people into the best restaurants. Just name it, and the following day, you're savouring lunch with Prime Ministers talking to your left and filthy rich entrepreneurs to your right.

"So," she said as she piled as much pasta as was possible onto a plate, "I'm just going to come out with it. What's happening?"

"I'm interested in Islam," I blurted out, and then mentally slapped myself. I thought I decided I was going to take this slowly. Oh bugger.

Her hand froze and for a full minute all was silent in our kitchen. With her eyes fixed on the plate, she spoke slowly, "I had no idea."

"It just happened recently. I didn't know myself until...a few days ago," I kept my eyes on her, wishing her to look at me.

She cleared her throat, "And are you going to go through with it?"

"I haven't made a decision yet. I'm a bit unsure but I hope to...," I started, just as she abruptly pushed away from the kitchen counter, turning her back to me, as the pasta spoon noisily clattered to the floor.

Without turning around, she said distantly, "I'm sorry but I'm not feeling so well anymore. I...I'm going for a walk. I'll be back soon." And with that she picked up her car keys from a nearby hook and walked out.

Speechless, I stood rooted to the spot, staring at her retreating back with startled eyes. I couldn't find it in me to eat and so I stared at the pasta until it had gone cold, as cold as my heart felt at that moment.

"How come the sun's yellow?" I ask, one hand propped under my head, as I lay on my back in our back garden. "I mean, why not some other colour? Why yellow?"

"Because yellow makes things look shiny and bright," Mum replies, from her position beside me, her eyes on the Vogue Magazine in her hand.

It's a typical Sunday morning, and as we soak in the sunlight, I engage in one of my favourite games; asking Mum questions that I know will be difficult to answer.

"That's a stupid answer."

"You loved it when you were five," she smiles slightly, and then turning her head to look at me lazily, asks, "What would you prefer? Pink?"

"No way," I say adamantly, horrified at the thought. At the age of seven, I'm the typical 'I-don't-want-Barbie- I-want-her-car' kind of girl. "I was just wondering."

"Why don't you ask God," she states.

"I would if I knew where He is."

Mum is silent for a moment, wondering how to answer back. "Okay, ask me again."

I grin slyly and turn on my side, facing her completely now. "Mum, how come the sun's yellow?"

"Because if it was pink, you'd go crazy and if it was blue, Jayne would go crazy. So it had to be a colour somewhere in the middle."

"God knows our favourite colours?" I ask in awe. And then before she can answer me, I let a wide grin take over my face and say, "Awesome."

She laughs loudly at that and says, "My turn. Who do you love more, me or Dad?"

"Mum, you can't ask that," I reply, as she puts the magazine away and sits up.

"Why not?" She takes out the chicken sandwiches that she made earlier and hands me one. "Eat."

"Can I have some Ribena first?" I ask.

"Food first, drinks later," she says, lying beside me again.

I take a bite out of my sandwich and stare up at the sky. After swallowing, I say, "Because you already know the answer."

"I do?"

"Yeah."

She's quiet for a moment. "I really don't think I do."

I sigh as I take in her wide grin, knowing that she's playing around. "Fine, I'll tell you but you can't tell Dad."

"Why not?"

"Because it'll break his heart," I say, as if it's the most obvious thing in the world. Dad has been super attached to me and Mark ever since he split up with Mum last year, and anyone can see that.

She looks confused now. "Why?"

"Because I love you more."

"You do?" she coughs, choking on her sandwich.

"Duh! You're my best friend. Miss Fanny said that men are always in and out of our lives but best friends are there forever. Dad's a man," I quip knowingly, "You can't tell Jayne either, because yesterday we made a pact that we'd be best friend's forever. Mum, does that make me a liar?"

Mum looks like she doesn't believe a word that is coming out of my mouth. She shakes her head and clears her throat, "I always thought you loved Dad more."

"Nope. So am I a liar?"

She just looks at me, and then slowly begins to smile. "No, you can always have two best friends. There's no rule that says you can't. "

"Phew."

Now we're both staring at each other, giggling for no reason, our legs stretched out on the warm grass. Mum's face is shining and I feel like mine is too.

"You look like a princess, mum."

"You are a princess, Kay."

That confession was nine years ago, and over the years I'd asked myself if I still felt that way, now I know that I did. Dad was the sort of person I'd miss, Mum was the sort of person I couldn't live without. But that day, I had also discovered something new, that Mum couldn't live without me either. She needed me, depended on me, and fortunately could never stay angry at me for too long. Miss Fanny had been right after all, best friends are there forever.

Knowing that my mum would forgive me sooner or later was probably the only reason why twenty minutes later I had left a note at home saying I was at the library. Being one of my favourite places in London, though, wasn't the reason I found myself at the library's reception desk, it was the fact that I knew this was the time to make a decision.

"Can I help you?" the girl behind the desk asked, taking in my unrecognizable, drenched form. Why hadn't I remembered to take an umbrella? "Wait, don't I know you?" she peered at me closely.

"Hi, Hannah," I smiled slightly, as she gaped at me. "Forgot my umbrella at home."

"*Katie?* Did you walk all the way here?"

"Yeah."

"Whoa," she said, staring at me with bug eyes.

"Listen, can you direct me to the err...Religion Section?"

Her eyes grew wider, if that was even possible, and she continued to stare at me incredulously.

"If you," I looked around uncomfortably, "happen to know where it is."

"Go through the Children Section, take a right, pass the Encyclopaedia Section, and it's straight ahead then," she spoke carefully.

As I turned to go, she couldn't help but ask, "Are you sure you wanna go there?"

Now it was my turn to look incredulous. "Why? Is it being guarded by mystical demons or something?" When she continued to look at me strangely, I sighed. "I wouldn't ask if I didn't want to go."

I found my way there in a matter of minutes, no mystical demons in sight. Fingering my way through the various Bibles, I finally chose the New Testament and pulled it out, then took a few more steps and pulled out the Quran. They both felt heavy in my hands as I carried them to a nearby table and sat down. I turned to the computer beside me and typed in my Library card number and logged in, figuring that at least this way if I didn't understand something I would be able to search the internet.

I looked down at the books in front of me and suddenly felt nervous; I had skimmed through the Bible a few times before when we were given study assignments but never opened it to see if what was written inside was actually the truth, and the Quran I was more than nervous to look through. I wiped my clammy hands on my jeans and resorted to surfing the internet first, my dad had told me of a website on which many Muslim converts

168

had written their stories and now I thought it would be good to take a look at them and see what points in their religion, mainly Christianity, didn't make sense to them.

I typed in the URL for the website, clicked enter and a couple of seconds later, found myself reading the strangest heading. 'Assalam-u-alaikum' it read, and beneath that 'May peace be on you'. Was that the way they greeted each other? It sounded so uncommon and quaint at the same time. I continued to read,

'In the Name of Allah, the Most Gracious, the Most Merciful. I will start with a small Du'aa - supplication to God.

'O Allah! Set right our religion that guards our souls from sins, make this world where we live better for us and make the Hereafter to where we return better for us, let life be a cause for more good and let death put an end to any evil that may befall on us. Let our hearts never go astray after You have guided us to the right path; endow us with Your Mercy. O Allah! You are our refuge when all doors are closed in our face, You are our hope when we become separated from our loved ones, You hear our supplications even before we utter them, we call You to let us live as Muslims and die as Muslims. La ilaha illallah, Muhammad Ar-Rasool Allah - There is no God but Allah and Muhammad is the Messenger of Allah.

'I hope this finds you in good health and high spirits of faith. Since a number of people are converting to Islam everyday - according to statistics, every year more than 200,000 individuals convert to Islam in the USA alone! - I've designed this website to be a guide for new Muslims as well as people who have not yet accepted Islam but are interested to. Here, you will find answers to your various questions, numerous stories and videos of fellow Muslim converts, and a detailed guide on what Islam is and how to accept it. As a former Catholic-Christian myself, I understand

the troubles that some new Muslims may face, and the questions that linger in the minds of non-Muslims. So please, if you have any questions, don't hesitate to visit the Q&A corner or contact me through the email given at the bottom of the page. I have especially put together a large variety of different convert stories which I hope will, InshaAllah - God Willing - help you to open up your heart to Islam and discover the beauty of the religion. SubhanAllah - Glorious is God.
Margaret A. Jones.'

I scrolled down and hesitated, wondering if I should start with the Q&A section, and then decided that I'd rather read the convert stories first, I was drawn to the idea that others might have felt like me at some point. I clicked on the 'Convert stories' tab and then looked on as a long list of Muslim and Christian names appeared, some with Muslim first names but Christian last names, and even some Hindu and Jewish names. I clicked on the first name, Aminah Assilmi, and began to read her story.

Chapter Seventeen

I blinked as the sound of running footsteps reeled me back into the present, to the library desk where I had been sitting for a good thirty minutes. One story had led to the next and the realization that so many people felt the way I did built up the more I read. I'd catch myself sometimes, wondering if this was all a dream but it wasn't. I could relate to all of these stories, the unanswered questions in Christianity, the need for united responsibility and pride in belonging to a religion, the simplicity of being able to turn to a God to guide you, and mostly that feeling of satisfaction in following and believing in the same God, the One True God.

I closed my eyes, as I remembered the many sentences that had touched me, *"Islam had a logic to it that I couldn't resist.", "I am astounded at how much I devour knowledge, how Islam is in my thoughts every waking moment, how compelling I feel my responsibility is to the Muslim nation and how much more of a Muslim I become every month.", "Everything I read was making sense.", "Finally, I was free.", "Islam has brought me a sense of peace and a sense of purpose that I never had before.", "I have established my identity, I am more confident of myself.", "I realized I would follow Islam at that point. I then became a Muslim. I knew the truth. I was out of the darkness.*

I came into the light.", "Everything seemed so clear now. It was almost like looking into a mirror. I saw my true self.", "It changed my goal from living in the moment to living with the intent of heaven.", "Islam has given me already so many vast rewards, I shiver to think of how much more wonderful the gifts of Paradise would be."

The unanswered questions in other religions was surprisingly the main reason why so many people turned towards Islam. *"When I was a Christian, I never understood why Jesus had to die for my sins. I mean, they're my sins.", "I turned to some verses about the prophets Lot and Solomon. God spoke of them as being noble prophets, unlike in the Bible. Even before this I could never understand how these people could commit such crimes as they were accused of in the Old Testament when they were the ones sent as examples for us.", "I had always questioned in my mind the concept of what Christians called the "Trinity" and why we had to pray to Jesus and not to God directly, and why so much emphasis was put on "Christ" and not God.", "Christianity was riddled with 'logical inconsistencies.'", "When I read the Quran, I knew for a fact that these could not be words of a man", "I didn't understand how babies could be born with original sin.", "The names "Christianity" and "Judaism" were not written in the Holy Scriptures. In fact, "Judaism" can be broken down into "Juda- ism" and "Christianity" could be respectively "Christ-ianity". These religions are named after people, the first was the tribe leader of the Hebrews when God revealed his message to mankind, the second was the person who delivered the message of God to the Jews. Therefore humans named them, not God. The notion that God would ordain a religion for mankind to follow without a name is impossible for my mind to accept. Islam is the ONLY one of these religions to include the NAME of the religion in its scriptures. "Indeed, the Religion in the sight of Allah is Islam..." (3:19)", "Strangely enough, the word "Trinity" is not in the Bible."*

I read how a person set out to destroy Islam but discovered the truth in it instead, how a former model/actress went from covering half of her body to covering her face, how a Swiss People's Party politician actively working against Islam suddenly came to accept it, how a woman accepted Islam and then helped convert thirty more people, how an aspiring rapper was moved by the image of a Muslim prostrating to God, how a young twelve-year-old boy growing up in the Caribbean saw the truth and accepted it wholeheartedly, and how a woman intent on finding the right religion for herself embarked on a long journey that in the end, after years of searching, lead her to the only true religion, Islam.

My eyes remained glued to the screen when I read that according to statistics, out of every five who convert to Islam, four are females. I'd always thought of Islam as a repressive religion for Muslim women, but now as I read these heart-warming stories, that concept was blown out of my mind, too hard to imagine. I found myself smiling as I read one woman's point of view, *"To women who surrender to the ugly stereotype against the Islamic modesty of Hijab, I say: You don't know what you are missing."*

It all seemed so beautiful, alluring even. *To know that there is a God out there to guide you, to watch over you, to know you inside and out and still love you.* To be your Protector, Sustainer, He who is the Lord of the Heavens and the Earth and all that is between it. Everything seemed so clear now, it was like looking into a murky pool of water as it cleared, and I could finally see my reflection.

But there was still one thing left, *the purpose of life* in Islam. And so I did the only thing that I could think of. I googled it. My eyes scanned the first few links and I decided to go with a small PDF article authored by a man named Khalid Yasin. It turned out to be eight pages long and like something I had never read before, it answered most of the questions that had been driving me mad for the past few days, explained the authenticity and miracles of the Quran, the message of the Prophets, the Oneness of God, and the meaning of Islam. And mostly, I found what I was looking for. There it was, right there, the purpose of life. And it was amazing.

'"*And I did not create the jinn and mankind except to worship Me.*" [Quran, Chapter 51: Verse 56] Our purpose in this life is to recognize the Creator, to be grateful to Him, to worship Him, to surrender ourselves to Him and to obey the laws that He has determined for us. Whatever we do in the course of that worship, [i.e. the eating, the sleeping, the dressing, the working, the enjoying] between birth and death is consequential and subject to His orders. But the main reason for our creation is worship.'

I understood what my dad had said about those Moroccan workers, leaving everything to go and worship God, I understood why all those people I had read about abandoned their former views and submitted to Islam, and I understood the wall hanging. I understood that all the questions in my head had actually only revolved around one, the purpose of life, and I felt something lift in my mind. It was extraordinary, I'd always thought that the feeling was fictional, an excuse to use a good expression, but really, *something lifted.* Something that had incessantly been troubling my mind was gone, replaced by something else, *peace*, a feeling that I had never felt as a Christian, and all I could think was '*I've found it!*'

I looked at the Quran now; in my eyes it mattered to me so much more than before, and laid a trembling hand on it, ready to begin reading the book that God revealed to mankind, His words and His guidelines.

As I began to open it, I suddenly heard a voice beside me, "Excuse me, Katie. I'm sorry but its closing time in five minutes. Would you like to purchase or borrow any books?"

"Oh, Hannah! You scared me there for a second." I half-jumped out my chair.

Steadying myself, I quickly remembered that she'd asked me something. "Yeah, I'd like to borrow this Quran if I could," I said, turning to log out of my account and then turning back to see her just standing there.

Her eyes immediately grew twice as large and her eyebrows were threatening to rise at any minute now. She blinked, glanced at the Quran in my hand, then at me, and then back again.

"But it's in Arabic," she managed to get out.

"No, this is a translation in English," I said, turning it over to show her the title. It began from the right side of the book, just like Arabic.

The lights began to dim for closing time, and she hastily pulled herself back together. "That would be no problem. Follow me."

I smiled slightly, and holding the Quran carefully in both hands, walked with her to the reception desk. The few people who were still at the library hadn't reached the reception desk yet and were still piling up books into their baskets, whilst one girl came up to stand beside me, leaning against the desk casually. She turned to glance at me, and began to smile until her eyes fell on the Quran in my hands, at which point she glared at me. At first I was surprised, and stared at her in confusion as she moved away, then I just grew irritated. *Really?* Was that glare supposed to make me feel insecure? Confidently, I put the Quran down on the counter, in clear sight of everyone, looked at Hannah straight in the eyes, and said, "Scratch out borrowing. I'd like to buy it."

It took less than three minutes for her to add 'Quran' to my list of books, take my signature and tell me to 'Please come back again soon', all the while maintaining the incredibly shocked look on her face that I was getting used to.

I reached home ten minutes later, and let myself into the house as silently as possible. Sure, it was only half eight, but with a reaction like that from a stranger I was more than worried about bumping into my mum. I tip-toed up to my room, shut the door quietly and took cover on my bed. Pulling out the Quran gently, I placed it in front of me and ran my hand across the beautiful Arabic inscription on the front cover, which in English read, 'The Noble Quran'. I let out the breath that I'd been holding in for too long, and began to read.

Anyone who knows me, who *really knows* me, will be able to tell you that once I've started a book it's impossible for me to put it down, besides 'Great Expectations' of course. No matter how long it takes me - and I must admit here that I'm an exceptionally fast reader, if I do say so myself - I finish reading the book, whether I'm in the car, or having lunch in the school dining hall, while sitting at the back of the class during a very boring lesson, or on the way to a jet-skiing trip, but mostly in bed at night. And last night was no exception; it took me exactly fifteen hours to read the entire translation of the Quran, all seven hundred and eighty-three pages of it.

It was the first time I had ever stayed up that long reading, and if it was any other book I might have felt proud of setting a new record, but instead as I turned over the last page the only feeling I felt was one of serenity. I had just read the most important book for all of mankind, a book revealed by God.

Every chapter, every verse had captured me, stimulated all sorts of emotions inside of me, at times I smiled with wonderment, just trying to imagine the beautiful descriptions of Heaven, and at times I shook with uncontrollable sobs and covered my mouth as the fear of living an eternity in the Hell Fire made it hard to breathe. I had felt an incredible sense of awe as I read verses that challenged mankind, verses that outlined the temporary beauty of this world in a way that I had never seen before, verses that answered questions even as they formed in my mind, verses that spoke to me. A few times I was even brought to a sudden halt, so amazed that I had to read the same verse over and over again.

"And when they (who call themselves Christians) listen to what has been sent down to the Messenger (Muhammad) you see their eyes overflowing with tears because of the truth they have recognized. They say: "Our Lord! We believe; so write us down among the witnesses." [Quran, Chapter 5: Verse 83]

"And We created not the heaven and the earth and all that is between them without purpose! That is the consideration of those who disbelieve! Then woe to those who disbelieve (in Islamic Monotheism) from the Fire!" [Quran, Chapter 38: Verse 27]

I cried when I read the heart-felt story of Prophet Abraham and his son Prophet Ishmael, I shivered when I read about the severe torture in the Hell Fire and God's wrath on the disbelievers, but what made my eyes water until I couldn't see a thing and frightened me so much that I had to gasp for breath was what I read in the following verse:

"And they will cry: "O Malik (Keeper of Hell)! Let your Lord make an end of us." He will say: "Verily, you shall abide forever." [Quran, Chapter 43: Verse 77]

Just the thought of a punishment so severe that it would make people cry for death, and the reality of it never ending made me convulse into sobs. There and then I felt a phenomenal change within me, and I knew that my outlook on life would never be the same again. Even before closing the Quran, I knew that I was Muslim.

Chapter Eighteen

I hurried downstairs and rushed into the kitchen, yanking the fridge open I quickly scanned the shelves for milk and then poured myself a glass, dumped two large tablespoons of Nesquick into it and managed to get to the kitchen counter without spilling a drop. I glanced at my watch for the fourth time as I gulped down the chocolate milk and then hungrily searched for something else to eat, my eyes zoning in on a chocolate muffin. It was quarter past twelve and I had already missed almost half of my lessons at school, but was ambitiously waiting for the sound of my dad's car pulling into the driveway any minute now. As I waited anxiously, I wondered when sleep would catch up with me, seeing as I'd yawned more than a handful of times already. Mum had left for work at her usual nine o'clock time so we hadn't spoken yet, but before I could worry about what I would say the next time I saw her, I heard a loud honk just outside the door. Taking a last bite out of the chocolate muffin in my hand, I ran outside to the car.

"Morning, Dad!" I chirped, hopping into the car.

He grunted, running a hand over his face sleepily, "Remind me again why Mark cancelled on you last minute?"

"Oh, he ended up pulling an all-nighter for some important exam he's studying for. Poor guy, he could barely talk to me over the phone before crashing onto his bed to sleep. Plus, I doubt he'd be capable to drive over from his university in the state he's in."

He looked at me, "How late are you?"

I glanced at my watch, "Approximately three hours and forty-eight minutes. I'll make it just in time for lunch break."

"Then why do you sound so chipper?" he muttered, reversing the car out of the driveway.

"Well," I laughed, "unlike *somebody's* sour disposal, I actually happen to be in a very good mood right now."

"You look exhausted," he said, as if that remark would have made any difference.

"But I feel great," I countered, eyes shining.

He stole a quick glance at my face, "Spill."

I grinned slowly, wondering how long I could prolong the moment, sucked in a breath dramatically and cried, "I'm Muslim!"

My dad's eyes grew in amazement, his face instantly breaking out into a wide smile, illuminating his entire face, "Wow! Are you serious? *Really?*"

"Yes, but I haven't said the exact words yet so can you —"

"Of course," he squeezed my hand, continuing to stare at me in wonderment. He recited the words one by one in Arabic, whilst keeping his eyes on the road, and I repeated them, a feeling of indescribable joy filling me.

"Ash hadu an laa ilaha ill Allah, wa ash hadu anna Muhammadan 'abduhu wa Rasooluh," I pronounced the words again, my eyes watery, my heart beating twice as fast. "I bear witness that there is no God but Allah and I bear witness that Muhammad is the Slave and Messenger of Allah."

My dad half-turned towards me, the grin on his face still there, as he excitedly asked, "How do you feel?"

"Happy, light, free," I laughed, and then just as suddenly began to yawn.

My dad chuckled, "Did you get any sleep at all?"

"Nope. I was up the entire night reading the Quran."

"*You finished it?* In one night!" he turned to gape at me.

"Dad, watch the road!" I exclaimed with a laugh. After a moment, having made sure that we weren't going to crash, I said softly, "Yeah, I did. It...it was so beautiful, *too beautiful* to put it down. I just couldn't."

I thought I saw tears in his eyes as he said, "Tell me everything. From beginning to end, I want to know how you became Muslim."

And I did. In that fifteen minute drive, I told him about Mum leaving the house, me trudging to the library in the rain, reading

181

convert story after story and the article on the purpose of life, how I dealt with the stranger's reaction, and finally how I felt when I read the Quran. I told him how Islam had changed my life from the very moment he walked into the house three weeks ago, and how I absolutely loved it.

"Wow! I can't believe it," Jayne cried, her jaw hanging open as she clutched my arm, her eyes wider than I'd ever seen before.

"Neither can I," I grinned.

"*When? How?* Tell me everything," she went on, moments after I had declared to her that I was Muslim.

I very readily recounted the story once again, explaining a few things here and there about Islam that Jayne didn't understand.

Lunch break had just ended and we were walking down the school hallway towards our next lesson, but nothing felt the same. For the first time, I actually noticed the Muslim girls walking around school, their headscarves a clear symbol of what they believed in. For the first time, I refused to join in the usual, belittling and gossip-filled talks at lunch and even snapped at Eva when she remarked on 'the audacity of those Muslims to ask Chef Jacques for a separate food menu'. For the first time, when I walked down the school hallways, guarding my secret in my heart, watching students pass me by, I thought, *'I'm Muslim'*. Everywhere I turned, every time I glanced at someone, the thought filled me completely, *'I'm Muslim'*, exciting me all over again.

"*So*," Jayne smiled secretively now, squeezing my arm, "I'm the first person you told, right?"

"Besides Dad, yeah."

She squealed and clapped her hands like a child.

Laughing loudly, I said, "Although, seeing you like this is making me rethink that now. I'm guessing that by the end of the day the entire school will be staring at me, and not because I'm wearing mismatched clothes."

She rolled her eyes as she gave me a slight shove, "I can keep a secret. Hello? Master of espionage here. And how did that happen? I've never seen you look so...*colourful*."

"I had two minutes to get changed and my mind was on other things. More important things, for that matter. And you know I'm sure that by Monday all the girls will be wearing blue shirts with red pants."

"Doubtful," she exhaled a half laugh, "so, how does it feel?"

"Like life has meaning to it," I said, "I can't even begin to describe to you how *amazing* that feels."

She smiled, "No need, I can see it all over your face. So, are you going to start wearing one of those...umm headscarf things?"

I nodded slowly, "I want to wear Hijab, of course I do, but

every time I think about it I feel this—" I grimaced, "—knot in my stomach. I mean, it's a big step and I had no idea I was so worried about what others would think. It's just...," I sighed, "once I wear it, everyone will know."

"True. But Kay, if what's holding you back is other peoples' views, then don't let it affect you and cloud your judgement. This is what *you want*, what *you believe in*. Nothing can stand in your way, and hey, I've got your back."

"Wow, you actually sounded philosophical for a second there," I spoke, with a new sense of awe for her, as she burst into laughter.

"Oh, yeah, baby. There's a whole side of me you've never seen," she joked.

I laughed, "Tell it to come out more often. Those pep talks actually help."

She grinned, "So, when are you going to spill the beans to Jeff?"

Suddenly, a flash of Jeff's smiling face flitted through my mind and I halted abruptly, almost bumping into the person behind me before Jayne swiftly pulled me out of the way.

"Whoa. Steady there. You almost knocked into the person –"

"*Jeff*," I looked at her with huge eyes, "Jayne, I haven't spoken to Jeff."

"Well, duh, I'm the first person you told."

"No, no, I mean, I *haven't spoken* to Jeff. At all."

Her mouth formed a big O as I relayed the message in her astonished eyes into words. "Oh my God."

"So, how does your mum feel about all of this?" Jayne asked, as we strolled towards the crowd of cars in the school parking lot, a few hours later.

The remainder of the lessons had whizzed by astonishingly fast, or perhaps only to me, as my mind continued to remain preoccupied with a thousand worrying and exciting thoughts for the rest of the school day.

I searched the cars in the parking lot for my dad's, and replied, "She doesn't know yet. I have no idea what she'll say, but I'm hoping it doesn't turn into a fight."

She laid a hand on my arm, "Look, don't worry. Just take it slowly, Ellie's a reasonable person, once she sees how much this matters to you, she'll be fine."

"I hope so," I said.

"Kay, everything will be fine. Believe me when I say, you're stronger than you think you are. Heck, you're stronger than I think you are," she grinned back.

I pulled Jayne into a tight hug, "Thanks for everything. I'll call you later."

I turned and made my way to my dad's car, immediately noticing the large grin on his face, even from yards away.

"Assalamu alaikum," my dad said as I approached him, taking my bag off me.

"Err, same to you?" I asked.

"Its 'Wa alaikum assalam'," he chuckled, "How was your day? Did I mention how glad I am that you're Muslim? I'm not sure if I told you enough times—"

"Oh, you did," I grinned, "And if only you could have seen Jayne's face when I told her," I shook my head in amusement.

"I think I can imagine it," he said with a slight smile, "What about Jeff? He must have been pretty surprised too."

"Oh." I blinked at the sudden change in topic, dropping my gaze quickly. "No, I haven't told him yet."

He raised his eyebrows, "Well…that's different."

I swallowed. I didn't want him to know about the falling out between Jeff and me, and so I decided to take the general route and confuse him.

"I just haven't thought about how to do it yet. I mean, I haven't even seen him around school much lately either and he's been pretty busy, and so have I, so there was never a time to well, you know, *tell* him. But I mean, I only became Muslim today, so who am I kidding? It's not that late… right?" I went on, pacing to my right and left now as my dad tried to interject, his eyes growing large and insistent, "I mean, how do I go about telling him

186

anyway? Do I avoid him and let him find out like everyone else or should I just spring it onto him? Like 'Hey, Jeff, how's life? *By the way*, I'm Muslim.'"

"You're *Muslim?*"

I spun around in shock as suddenly the very topic of our conversation came into view. Jeff. *How long had he been standing there?*

"I was trying to warn you," my dad mumbled, just low enough for me to hear, before beaming at Jeff and speaking loudly, "Well, hey, my back's beginning to ache because of…umm standing this long, so I'm just going to head back into the car," he took a step back, "and *rest* my…back. So I'll be here. Just here. In err…the car. Waiting for…well, I'll leave you two to it," he waved, before slipping into the car, and shutting the door noisily.

We stood there awkwardly for a moment as Jeff realized that he still hadn't wiped the shocked look off of his face, and then hurriedly did so. I looked down at my shoes and waited for him to say something, but when he didn't, I peeked up to see that he was still staring at me with a strange expression. Dumbfounded, almost. It had been almost a week since we'd last spoken, and it felt surreal that now that we were finally in front of each other, everything had changed so drastically. I was Muslim now.

Realizing that the silence was getting us nowhere and that I didn't quite like being under the spotlight, I took it as my cue to speak.

"Hey, Jeff," I spoke in a blasé tone, shrugging my shoulders casually like I'd seen Mark do when he was trying to get out of trouble, "What's new?"

187

When he didn't reply, I mentally smacked my head. *Why am I imitating Mark of all people?* Okay, Katie, be yourself. Easy. Just, *be yourself.*

"I'm Muslim," I blurted out. Okay, *don't be yourself, stay clear away from being yourself!*

"Yeah, I kinda figured. You were quite clear before," he said, finally recovering from his shock.

"I was gonna tell you."

"You've been avoiding me."

"No, I haven'—"

"*Yes*, you have," he said in a highly annoyed manner.

"I didn't want to get my emotions involved…with my decision," I declared, crossing my arms.

"What do you mean?" he cocked his head.

"Just that you're my…," I paused. It was time to take the first step, to leap off the cliff, to restore the bridge, and to fix the pieces of the puzzle in my life. So I took a deep breath and said, "My best friend."

"So is Jayne."

I blinked. I hadn't expected that. "Well, Jayne's different," I said with exasperation. "She's a *girl.*"

He looked at me for a long moment, "I see."

What did that mean? Wait, had I just declared something about myself? About my feelings?

"Not that it makes much of a difference or anything," I quickly corrected.

"I'm sure it doesn't," he agreed, sounding suspiciously amused.

"And you were right," I declared, in an attempt to change the subject, "About everything. About accepting change and about finding peace."

He dropped his gaze to the ground and shook his head, "I was a jerk. I was too harsh and stupid and was blinded by my own feelings for—" he halted, turning slightly red.

"Yeah?"

"Nothing," he mumbled, and then raised his head, a slightly boyish grin on his face, "So am I forgiven?"

"As long as you forgive me for acting like a drama queen."

He grinned, "Deal. Boy, were you a drama queen."

"Jeff Collins, don't you make me—"

"And hey, I was never really angry at you," he interrupted, "Just concerned. Although, you can be pretty stubborn sometimes," he raised his hand before I could interject, "actually, *most* of the time." I rolled my eyes, as he continued, "But that's what I admire about you."

I blinked. Okay, rewind. What had I just missed?

"You're strong headed, Kay, and you don't let anyone or anything get in between you and what you believe in."

"Oh. Well, I...," I shuffled my feet, "I was steered in the right direction by some guy I know."

He grinned. "So what changed your mind about Islam?"

"Dad. I stopped running away from him and embraced him into my life again. After that, things sort of changed between us. He seemed much happier than before and it was obvious he was dying to tell me about Islam," I smiled, "so I did the only thing I could in that situation. I listened."

"And then he converted you?" he looked astonished.

"No, I...I needed to discover it for myself, so I did my own research. When I read the Quran, that was my final turning point. I couldn't deny that it was," I hesitated, wondering if I sounded like I was lecturing him, "the truth," I finished.

He broke his gaze away and frowned, looking deep in thought for a moment.

"Jeff?"

He looked up, "Oh. Yeah, well, that's great, Kay. Great to hear. I better get going though. I've got some... things to do."

I looked away quickly. Right. Of course. "Yeah, me too. Dad's waiting in the car...," I turned my head to see that he was in fact very happily amusing himself with the seat's elevation system, reclining it backwards and then zooming back up again with quick speed.

190

Jeff smiled slightly, "Yeah, you better go, before he really does hurt his back."

I looked up at him with surprise, and he just nodded at me. "So, I guess I'll see you later, Kay?"

"About that," I swallowed, realizing that this may be the last friendly conversation I'd have with Jeff. "See in Islam, Muslims aren't supposed to free-mix. As in, girls and boys don't errm… freely form friendships with one another. As in they don't just hang out. And I respect that," I recalled what Sarah had said at the dance, *It's as pure a religion as any can be.* "So, I…," I took a deep breath, "I can't…you'll always be my best friend, but I can't…."

"I understand," Jeff spoke softly, and for a moment I wanted to cry.

He sometimes knew me better than I even knew myself. My dad had told me before that taking this step would be hard, but I'd pushed it to the back of my mind for later, thinking that when the time would come, I'd be ready. Now the time was here and I could barely utter a proper goodbye as Jeff looked at me one last time and walked away. I guess, when it really comes down to it, you can never prepare yourself for heartbreak, no matter how big or small it is.

Chapter Nineteen

"So, how did it go with Jeff?" Dad asked cautiously, a few minutes later, having finally chosen the best possible position for his seat.

"It was…interesting," I replied evasively, looking outside the window. It had begun to rain and oddly enough, as my eyes followed the raindrops on my window, I suddenly recalled one of my favourite childhood memories with the Collins twins.

"Hah! Gotcha again. That's three points for me and—" I said pompously when all of a sudden a water bomb splat into my face. I was hurled back a few steps and my eyes grew in shock as Jeff laughingly emerged from behind the bushes.

"You spoke too early, Kay. Now we're even," he grinned, smugly bouncing another water bomb up and down in his palm.

Out of the corner of my eye, I noticed Jayne carefully creeping up behind him and smiled broadly, "You were saying?"

Splat!

My jaw dropped open as Jayne stood soaked with water having suddenly been targeted by Jeff who spun around with spider-man reflexes.

"Jeff!" she shrieked.

Jeff turned around triumphantly, "I'm the King of the game. Admit it."

"Never," I retorted, crossing my arms in front of me, and sticking out my tongue like any other ten-year-old my age would do.

"Fine, then, you'll just have to suffer the consequences."

"Pfft. What consequences?" I rolled my eyes.

"He likes using big words," Jayne teased, shaking her eleven-year-old head as she squeezed water out of her shirt.

"Tell me about it," I replied.

He fished out a camera from his pocket and aimed it at me, "Oh, you know, just the fact that this hilarious picture will circle around school in no time," then clicked the shutter button.

I gasped, "You wouldn't dare!"

He grinned, "I so would."

I narrowed my eyes at him and then suddenly smiled brightly, shrugging my shoulders, "All right."

A look of victory covered Jeff's face as he shot Jayne a smug smile and said, "Okay, then, come out with it. You have to say it loud and clear so everyone can hear. Or, maybe, you should just scream it, or better yet—"

"No, I meant all right, send the picture around," I challenged him, knowing even as a ten-year-old that Jeff would never hurt me that way.

Jeff paused mid-sentence and swallowed, "I will. I totally will. I've got the camera right here," he held it up again.

"Okay, your choice," I shrugged again, and then with the talents of an Oscar-winning actress, feigned sorrow, "I mean, it's totally in your hands if you want to ruin my image at school," I looked up at him with puppy eyes, "which would also ruin my chances of having friends," I sniffed and turned my face away, "which would mean ruining my life as well."

"Yeah, well…," Jeff started, unsure as what to say, "I guess I could uhh….give you some mercy this time….hey, wait, Katie, are you crying?"

My shoulders shaking up and down with laughter, I shook my head, even as a giggled slipped out suddenly which I hastily changed into a whine.

"Whoa! Sorry, you know I didn't really mean any of that, right?" Jeff asked with concern, stepping forward tentatively.

Wanting to get a good look at his concerned face, I raised my head up, with my hands covering my face, and immediately noticed Jayne creeping up behind him a second time, this time with a hose in her hand! Jeff was too preoccupied with making sure that I was all right to notice her approaching him. Catching the gleam in her eyes, I snorted loudly, as Jeff's eyes grew in shock and at the same time water blasted out of the hose, soaking him in an instant.

Removing my hands from my face, I doubled over in laughter, as Jayne manically directed the hose at him, even as he turned away and shielded himself with his hands. I continued to laugh as she got closer to him, when unseeingly out of nowhere, his hand shot out and seized the hose, pulling it out of her grasp. Her eyes widened in horror as she hurriedly stumbled away from him, and he straightened up, hand on the hose, his eyes on me.

I shook my head, warning him with my eyes, as I too began to back away.

"You were laughing," he stated, coming closer.

"No," I held my hands up in surrender, backing away cautiously, "I was….giggling." I whipped around lightning-fast and ran for all I was worth, laughing at the top of my lungs, as he chased after me with the hose.

"You are so dead, Katie Anderson! Believe me, next time I won't give you any mercy! Just see!"

As I ducked and dived away from him that day, enjoying myself immensely, I knew with surety that whatever happened after that, he would never purposefully hurt me, he was my friend for life and after all, he'd threatened me countlessly before but never followed through.

"First reactions are always the best," my dad said, suddenly bringing me back to the present, "well, sometimes."

I smiled slightly, knowing that he was trying to divert my attention, and went along with it anyway. "You should have seen your face when I bolted from the car that day, Dad. Classic!"

He wasn't smiling as he replied, "I'm glad you can laugh about it now. For me, it wasn't all that. I honestly thought that was it, that you'd shut me out of your life and I'd never hear from you again," his voice dipped low at the end.

I looked down in embarrassment, "I'm sorry, Dad." I tried to imagine what it must have felt like as he watched me run away from him that day, for the first time.

"I always knew you'd apologize about it someday, though," he said cheerfully, "Light at the end of the tunnel."

I swung my head up to find his eyes filled with laughter and his mouth pulled up in a broad grin. "I can't believe you!" I laughed, shaking my head, "Manipulating me into feeling sorry for you. You, *mister*, had the far better end of the stick. *I* was the one who ended up with a bloody knee."

"If the far better end of the stick means being left with a broken, shattered heart," he spoke dramatically, "compared to just a...what was it you said? Bloody knee?"

"You're unbelievable," I said, unable to stop myself from grinning.

"Well, I guess I might be exaggerating just a little bit," he joked, and then his voice took on a softer tone as he added, "I prayed every night you know, that you'd come to see the truth or at least let me back into your life. And then you called out of the blue, asking me to pick you up from a party, and if only you could have seen my face *then*. The only dad who could have been that happy to pick his daughter up from a party past midnight."

"You were the first person I thought of, Dad. I couldn't imagine…life without you."

"Same goes for you," he said, as we turned into my street, "I can't stop counting my blessings. The amount of incredible stuff that has happened this week! You accepting me back into your life and not just that, but *becoming Muslim*, Markie getting accepted into Oxford, my architectural project in Morocco being such a hit that they want me to do a whole series there over the next couple of years. Wow. All I can say is *Alhamdulillah - All praise is for Allah*!"

"Whoa, whoa, wait. Rewind. *Mark got into Oxford?* But how...he's already halfway through his first term of university," I exclaimed.

"Yeah, he called just before I came to pick you up. Apparently, his professor thought his academic level was too high for the class he was sitting in, and put in a good word for him when speaking to a friend at Oxford. That friend just happened to be one of the *coordinators* at Oxford, and let him sit the admission exam! He passed and that's all there is to it. He got a scholarship too. The boy's a genius. He's shifting after his mid-terms," he spoke excitedly, and then after a moment's thought, added in, "I hope it wasn't a surprise."

"Wow! No wonder he was stressing out over the past few days. Don't worry dad, whatever happens, I'll act surprised," I said, just as we reached home.

"So, you still haven't told me what you want to do this weekend. We could go white-water rafting or kayaking, I know this brilliant place outside London, somewhere in North Wales," his eyes glinted as he turned off the ignition and faced me.

"What is it with you and water, Dad?" I asked.

"Having been a fantastic lifeguard when I was your age might have something to do with it, or the fact that I practically grew up in the sea," he grinned all over his face. "When I was six, I was constructing sandcastles that were worthy of being as acclaimed as...the Mona Lisa."

"Yeah right," I laughed, "Actually, this time I have something else in mind, but it's a surprise," I unbuckled my seatbelt, "I'm going to go inside and get my stuff, be back in five."

I stepped out of the car and skipped towards the front door as he wailed, "You know I hate surprises!"

"Which is why it's all the more fun!" I yelled back.

I entered the house with a sunny glow spread across my face, unable to hold in the excitement of my conversion any longer. I hummed happily as I padded into the kitchen, only to be stopped short by the sight of my mum sitting at the kitchen counter, staring blankly at the un-touched food in front of her. She looked up at the exact moment I strolled in, a stunned expression passing over her face as she absorbed the breathless smile on mine. Stupefied, I stood there awkwardly, attempting to wipe the smile clean off my face.

"Mum! What are you doing here?"

The initial shock still hadn't left her face, as she cautiously said, "The girls were doing fine at the hair salon so I came home early."

"Oh," I furrowed my brow, trying to remember the last time that had happened, if ever.

"Did you have a good time at school today?" she asked, suddenly sounding more on edge.

At the sound of her tone, my smile vanished completely, "It was okay."

"You look like you did. Had a good laugh with your fr—"

"I'm Muslim," I interrupted her quickly, my face passive, not giving away any emotions. Better to get this over and done with now, I thought detachedly.

A horrified expression took over her face, as her gaze swept all over me, looking for any signs that I might not be telling the truth, her eyes searching mine intensely. She seemed unaware of the sudden shaking that had taken over her hands and the paleness that had crept across her face. I wanted to scream, to shout, *anything* to stop the alarmed expression that haunted her face.

The unexpected honking sound from my dad's car abruptly broke the silence.

"That's Dad," I managed to whisper.

She closed her eyes and then opened them again, the look of alarm drastically disappearing, and I wondered if she was hoping this was a bad dream, but was taken-aback when she suddenly forced a smile, "Th....that's great. Good for you. I....I hope you're happy."

"I am," I returned a hesitant smile, my thoughts turning to Islam.

She wiped at her eyes as they filled with tears, "I....I'm just overwhelmed, that's all. This is great. Just great."

I wanted to comfort her but instead I found myself frozen in place, "I was just going to grab my stuff."

"Oh, yes, you're spending the weekend with your dad. That's good. Yeah, just take your stuff and have a good time," she nodded at me, her eyes moving towards the plate in front of her again.

"Is Mark going to—"

"Be here? Yeah, yeah. Jack's waiting, you should go. Take care of yourself and...," she paused, her eyes meeting mine fleetingly, "just don't forget who you are Katie."

I was confused at the last part, not entirely sure what she meant, but reassured her anyway. I stumbled up towards my room, the change in my mood visible in the way I hunched my shoulders slightly. I looked around for anything I might need, an assignment I had to finish, my phone charger, my camera case. It's funny how once your parents have divorced, you don't need to bother with essentials like toothbrushes or shampoo when staying with them since you'll have a spare there anyway, it's like living two separate lives in a way. I traced my steps back towards the front door, pausing in the kitchen on my way to give my mum a proper goodbye, something which I was taught to do ever since I was a child. No matter how bad the argument I just had to wrap my arms around her once before leaving the house.

When I reached the car, I noticed my dad had inclined his chair backwards *again*, laid his arms behind his head and shut his eyes. I quietly sat in the car, pulled my seatbelt on as slowly as possible and then fastened it with a soft click, turning my head to make sure the door was locked.

I bumped my head on the roof of the car when suddenly my dad muttered, "I didn't know five minutes constituted of half the day, Katie."

"Ouch," I rubbed my head, "I bumped into Mum."

"She was home?" he asked with surprise, shifting into a sitting position once more, and then tilted his head at me, "You don't look very happy anymore."

I remained silent as he pulled the car out of the driveway, and then couldn't manage to keep it in any longer and mumbled, "She came home early, and no, it didn't go so well."

"Are you going to tell me what happened?"

"Why do I have such a big mouth?"

"You inherited that from your great grandmother. Maternal, may I add," he quipped.

My mouth twitched as I said haughtily, "I know fully well that I do not have a big mouth, *what I meant* was that why can't I ever

201

think before blurting something out?"

"Now *that's* from my side," he winked at me.

"Da-ad!"

"So you told her?"

"Well, yeah, I blurted it out. I can't keep things from Mum, everyone knows that," I put my head in my hands.

"Kat—" he started.

"—and it was horrible," I lifted my head, "she made this face like she...she just wished this was happening to someone else."

"Katie—"

"— and she looked so hurt and I wish, I just wish that—"

"*Stop*. Katie, stop," my dad pulled the steering wheel forcefully to the right and the next thing I knew we had skidded to a stop on the side of the road. "Don't even go there. Tell me this, do you believe in God?"

I stared at him as if he was crazy, "What does that have to do with any of this?"

"Answer the question."

"Yes, of course. I think I made that kind of clear when—"

"Do you trust Him?"

I nodded affirmatively when I realized he wouldn't let me get a word in.

"Do you believe that no matter what happens He will always be there for you?"

I paused, hesitating. I had never been one to rely on others easily, and it had taken years for me to form strong relationships as a child with others, especially after the shock of my parents' divorce. Mark had been my shield after that, the only one who understood what I was going through, and Jayne and Jeff, well they had been there from the beginning anyway. So, I knew that putting my trust in people had not always reaped good results, but putting my trust in *God*, well that was another matter. That I could try, and *that*, I was sure would reap a whole different type of result. "Yes."

"Good, that's all you need to keep in mind. Peoples' disparaging opinions, views and feelings don't matter when it comes to you and your connection with God. It all comes down to what *you* believe in and how firmly you trust in His will and power to make everything else fall into place. Ellie's your *Mum*, your mentor, your best friend, your whole world, and I guarantee that it will hurt, it will cause you real pain if she doesn't come to accept you. But at the end of the day, everything that happens is by His will, so all you can really do is put your trust in Him and hope for the best," he looked at me kindly, "and I will add in this. Ellie loves you to bits, and the person that she is just wouldn't be capable of causing you any sort of pain, so I also guarantee that it will be amazing, fantastically wonderful if she does come to accept you. From here on, it all depends on her understanding just how important this is to *you*, and for that you're going to have to show her, you're going to have to *be a Muslim*. And you'll need Allah's help every step of the way, so trust in Him, do your best, and let

Allah do the rest."

Everything he said sounded amazing, to the point that I had begun to tear up, so I smiled a wobbly smile and said, "Okay."

He chuckled, "Oh, I'm good. So will you please tell me about your surprise now?"

"Well, believe it or not, but this weekend you're going to teach me how to *be a Muslim*," I grinned.

Chapter Twenty

The doorbell rang shrilly and I strolled towards the front door, wondering who it could be. I swung it open to find myself looking at a short, Asian man, with a load of bags in his hand, weighing him down as he puffed, "That'll be thirty pounds, plus tip, please."

I smiled, took the bags from him, and said, "Hang on a minute." Walking into the kitchen, I laid the bags onto the counter and took a quick peek inside at the food. "Dad! You ordered Thai!"

My dad winked at me as he walked past me towards the front door, thanked the deliverer, addressing him by his first name, *Ping*, and paid him. He strolled back into the kitchen, "Occasions call for fancy food."

"But Mango Tree doesn't even deliver," I replied, as I munched on a mouthful of Papaya salad.

"I have my ways. Think of this as a treat for working so hard," he smiled.

It was seven o'clock, and I'd just spent the past few hours hard at work, learning how to perform the daily prayers, among other things. The first step was ablution, a step-to-step washing up that was necessary for reading the Quran and performing the daily prayers, after that I learnt the different steps in prayer and the Arabic verses recited in them. It was tough, especially since Arabic was an entirely new language, and I'd only been able to remember a couple of them. My dad made sure to give me a handful of CD's to listen to at home along with a promise to teach me how to read Arabic, something he was still learning himself. He also taught me a variety of necessary Du'aas - supplications to God - which I could use daily, described the beauty behind the *Hijab* - headscarf, explained the prohibitions in Islam, and the importance of living according to Islamic guidelines.

I hung onto every word, and absorbed as much of the information as I could in the space of a few hours. Then my dad suggested we cool off by playing some video games, and much to his surprise, I very smugly beat his high score in the first ten minutes. After that it was war, with him pounding his fists on the floor every time I neared his score, and whooping loudly when he was close to winning. He'd just been about to reclaim the highest score, when the doorbell rang and I jumped up elatedly to answer it, putting an end to the game. Now I relaxed, savouring the delicious Thai food in front of me, proud of how much I'd learnt and thirsty for more.

My dad seated himself opposite me, uttering "*Bismillah*" before taking a bite out of his Pad Thai Noodles.

I stopped chewing momentarily and then swallowed quickly, "What does that mean?"

"It means 'In the Name of Allah' and you say it before eating, or starting something new."

I nodded my head, "It makes sense. So, what are we doing tomorrow?"

"Do you have anything in mind or can I reveal *my* surprise?"

I smirked, "It's pretty obvious dad. White water rafting."

"Well, I had a Muslim party in mind, an introduction to the Muslim society for you and a night of barbecue-ing for me, but if you're more inclined to that then…," he trailed off.

"*When?* Tomorrow? What time? Am I invited?"

"Yes, tomorrow," he laughed, taking in my anxious expression, "six in the evening, and would I be asking you to come if you weren't?" He took in my look of obvious confusion and carried on, "After dropping you off at school, I was on the phone with one of my close friends, Yousuf, and mentioned to him that you had just become Muslim. He's one of the few who knows about my relationship with you and Mark. He told his wife and she immediately asked him to invite you to the barbecue at their house tomorrow. I hadn't been planning to go since I thought we'd do something fun this weekend, maybe white-water rafting," he winked at me, "and then their invitation to you came up and I just knew it would appeal to you more."

"But…but…she hasn't even met me," I said, flabbergasted.

"To her, you're a new Muslim sister, and that's enough reason."

I was touched, "That's sweet. I just hope I don't disappoint anyone, I mean I'm still new to all of this. I don't know the ins and outs and…"

"You won't. A lot of the sisters have actually been through more or less the same struggle as you. Some of them are reverts, like us, and some of them were born Muslim but changed their lives around and—"

"Wait, what did you just say?" I interrupted.

"That some of them are like us, reverts," he spoke slowly, a rising intonation at the end of his voice.

"No, no, that part about born Muslims. You said that they *changed their lives around?* What do you mean?" I asked eagerly, recalling Sarah's confession to me about her desire to change.

"That they repented for their past sins and changed themselves; the company they were with, their sinful actions, to put it simply, their way of life. They turned back to Allah for guidance and help," he said.

"And He forgave them?"

"Well, yes, if they were sincere in their repentance then He did. One of the most beautiful attributes of Allah is that He is All-Forgiving. Whatever sin you've committed vanishes if you repent to Allah sincerely."

"Wow, that's amazing."

"Yeah, and you'll get to meet some sisters who have gone through that, who now live for the Hereafter. Some of them have daughters your age as well, so I think they might be able to help you with the idea of *Hijab* and relate to you more," he smiled encouragingly.

It sounded amazingly exciting and terrifying at the same time. I took a deep breath, "Well, I've never been to a Muslim party before. What's it like?"

He grinned, "Just wait and see."

"Are you sure I look all right?"

"Positive."

I was nervous, more than nervous, petrified. "I'm not wearing a *Hijab*. What if they look at me weird?"

It was exactly four o'clock and we were parked directly outside Yousuf's house on Elm Tree Road, deep in the heart of St. Johns Wood, as my dad tried to calm my nerves and I sat rigidly on my seat. I had no idea what to imagine of the people I was about to meet, not a clue. My dad wasn't much help, seeing as he had only spent time with the men and described them as 'nice, laidback fellows with a great sense of humour'. I imagined it at its worst, women eyeing me, staring at me the entire evening, whispering about me, labelling me the 'new girl', and just the thought of that made me want to turn back and spend the evening at home.

"Honey, of course they won't think that. You're not the first Muslim girl they've come across who isn't wearing a hijab. Unfortunately, there are others like that out there who *make* that their choice in life, fooled by the glamour of this world into ignorance of their own religion."

I thought about Sarah again and understood his point. "Yeah, but I don't want them to think I'm like that."

He smiled at me guiltily, "And there's the fact that you just reverted yesterday morning, and your silly father didn't think of buying you one."

"You're not silly, you were just giving me some space," I smiled, giving in, "Fine, we'll go in, but if I don't like it I'll call you and we'll leave straight away, okay?"

"Yes, Ma'am."

I stepped out of the car, smoothing down the knee-length blue and white checkered top I was wearing, something I normally would have worn by itself in the summer but had now paired with denim jeans and a white cardigan. It had taken me a full ten minutes rooting in my wardrobe to find a pair of decent loose-fitting jeans to wear, and even longer to find a cardigan, undoubtedly I had to buy a new wardrobe of clothes soon.

My dad walked up to me with a heart-warming smile on his face, jokingly offering me his arm as if he were about to walk me down a wedding aisle, and I chose that moment to ask, "Dad, when I was leaving the house yesterday, the last thing Mum said

210

to me was, 'Don't forget who you are'. I've been trying to make sense of it ever since but I can't, I don't understand...what did she *mean*?"

He thought for a moment, "I think she meant that whatever happens, don't forget that Katie Anderson can do whatever she puts her mind to, and that in the most difficult times she can still stay strong."

My mouth pulled up into a smile as I said, "I think you're right."

"And *I* think that everybody in there must be wondering what a crazy lot we are for standing out here for this long."

"Really?"

"No."

I laughed and tugged on his hand, "Come on, we better go inside."

My dad stopped just before I reached the door and said, "Men are in the back garden, women are in the house."

"Oh. Yeah, that's something I still have to get used to. Well, wish me luck," I said, not letting go of his hand.

"Have fun," he said instead, squeezing my hand and walking away with a wave.

"I'll try," I mumbled, working up my courage as I lifted my finger to ring the doorbell, a friendly smile plastered onto my face.

I heard a clatter of running footsteps approach the door and then a young, girly voice sang from the opposite end, "*Who is it?* Hamza, no! Stop it! *I'm* going to open the door!"

"Umm... Katie," I replied.

"Katie who?" she sang again, sweetening her voice and then yelling shrilly, "Hamza! *Stop it!*"

Before I could reply with my full name, I heard a young woman's voice call out, "Zaynab! Hamza! Get *away* from the door please! No, neither of you can....I'm sorry but it's mummy's turn."

The door opened a second later, revealing the smiling face of the young woman, and two small heads as the children peeked out from behind her. "Assalam u alaikum. You must be Katie! Come in, come in."

I smiled hesitantly as I stepped in, "Wa alaikum assalam. Yeah, that's me."

"Oh, wow. You're beautiful. MashaAllah TabarakAllah," she said, her chocolate brown eyes shining.

I blushed as I recognized the term used for praising someone or something, by giving due praise to Allah first. Even though I'd been told this all my life, no one had ever been this direct to me. "So are you," I replied shyly, as I handed her the homemade Oreo truffles I'd brought. And I meant it, with a pair of large brown eyes, glossy black hair pulled back into a messy ponytail, and creamy white complexion she looked effortlessly beautiful.

"JazakAllahu Khair," she grinned, thanking me as she pushed away strands of hair from her face, "with four wild kids running around the house I didn't really get time to do much."

"*Four?*" I asked incredulously. Imagining her with two kids was hard enough; she looked about twenty-three.

"Yup. And what a handful they are; Khadija, Fatima, Zaynab, and Hamza. Poor Hamza's stuck with three bossy older sisters," she smiled down at him, patting his head lovingly.

"I have two bossy older sisters," Zaynab piped up.

"Yes, you do," her mum laughed, "how about you go and set up your new dollhouse to show your friends later? Yusra will be here soon for you to play with."

Zaynab's eyes lit up and she ran off in the other direction, with Hamza waddling after her.

She turned to me, "That's what happens when you get married at eighteen."

"*Eighteen?*"

"Yeah, been married eight years now," there was a certain sparkle in her eyes as she added, "and somehow I don't think I would have wanted it any other way."

"Wow."

She blinked, "Oh my! I'm so sorry, I didn't even introduce myself properly. Here I am going on about my life story....my name's Habiba, I'm Yousuf's wife," she held out her hand.

I grinned and shook it, "You already know my name."

213

"So I'm searching everywhere for my baby bag and then bingo, I realise that I left it in the car. Do you have any nappies? Lamya just peed her pants," I heard a voice, just as a stunning young woman turned the corner. I had never seen anyone look that fabulous in an oversized yellow 'SpongeBob Square Pants' shirt before. Her skin was a glowing olive complexion, and long eyelashes framed her beautifully shaped brown eyes. Her mouth was pulled up into an exasperated grin, and her shoulder length jet black hair stuck out from different angles in a jazzy style, accentuating her cheekbones and giving her a look that no one else could have pulled off any better. "Oh. You must be Katie."

"Isn't she stunning?" Habiba asked.

"Yeah," we both replied at the same time.

I blushed once again, as she grinned at me and shook my hand, "Assalam u alaikum. I'm Samra. How are you?"

"Great."

"That's good. Normally Habs scares people off the first time she meets them," she winked at me.

Habiba rolled her eyes, a hint of a smile tugging at her lips, "That only happened once, with *you*."

"She burst into tears right after I said my Salam."

"I had lost the twins in Hyde Park, so it was perfectly all right for me to run around like a headless chicken," she explained to me and then turned to Samra, "Nappies are in the top cupboard in the playroom, you'll find some baby wipes in there too."

214

"I hate potty-training. It was very nice to meet you, Katie. I'll tell you the entire story later," Samra said, grinning as she walked off in the other direction, and then yelled, "Habs, are the cupcakes done yet? I'm starving!"

Habiba's eyes popped open wide, "Oh my god, I forgot the cupcakes!" and then she ran to the kitchen at full speed.

I muffled a laugh as I followed her into her brightly lit, woodsy kitchen and watched as she took the cupcakes out with a 'Barney' baking glove. I looked around at the kitchen, noticing the paintings and alphabet magnets on the fridge, the colourful Ikea plates and boxes of 'Nesquick' cereal on the kitchen counter, and the words 'Always say 'Bismillah' before eating' written in colourful felt-tip pens, on a paper taped to the wall.

"Oh, Alhamdulillah! They're just perfect. Want one?" Habiba offered me a cupcake.

"JazakAllahu Khair," I smiled, repeating the words she'd used before, and helped myself to one. My eyes grew, "These are incredible."

"Yeah, somehow she's the messiest, craziest cook but her food comes out utterly delicious," Samra said from the door as she approached us, a little girl in her arms now.

"Is that your daughter?" I exclaimed with shock, taking in the toddler's light tan, curly brown hair and hazel eyes.

She smiled knowingly, "None of my kids resemble me much. They've all gone on their Spanish father."

I looked at both of them, "Where are you both from?"

"She's originally Pakistani, and I'm originally Palestinian, but we grew up here our entire lives. Friends since university," Habiba commented as she slipped an apron on and began decorating the cupcakes. "Sam, we're not even introducing ourselves properly. What must she think?"

Samra grinned, "Okay then, Habs here, is a mother of four. She's the clumsiest person you'll ever meet, she has a mad addiction for cheesecakes but never puts on even a pound, she's terrified of cats and is the worst Arabic teacher I've ever had."

Habiba looked up with a sly smile, pushing her hair back from her face and in the process leaving a long line of pink icing on her cheek, and retorted, "While, Sam here, is a mother of three of the cheekiest kids I have ever had the pleasure to meet and is expecting her fourth," I turned to Samra with a surprised grin. She looked anything but pregnant right now as she perched on a kitchen stool, actively bouncing Lamya up and down on her knee, whilst still managing to sip her coffee. "She's the most straight-forward person you'll ever meet, she's passionately in love with all languages but has the most terrible Arabic accent, and has a weakness for homeless cats."

I laughed, "You're both hilarious." I couldn't believe how well this was going. So far, I hadn't been stared at, whispered about or labelled. In fact, judging by the past five minutes I was pretty sure I was having a fabulous time.

Habiba grinned, "Wait till you meet the others."

I blinked, "Others?"

The doorbell rang and Habiba yelled, "I'm coming!" before rushing off in her apron to the door.

Samra laughed at my expression, "Eight more families to be exact. Don't worry, we don't bite."

I smiled back nervously as I followed Samra into the living room and heard Habiba greet the guests that had just arrived. "Assalam u alaikum, Aasiyah. How are you? Here, let me take that from you. Mmm, black forest cake, my favourite. Hello, Christy, how has everything been?"

Christy? Could it be? I imagined it for a moment and then shook my head, a self-mocking smile growing on my lips; this is the last place Christy would ever be on a Saturday night.

"Come on in, we've got a new sister here with us," I heard her continue as she turned the corner, two women following. Hang on a minute, one was a *girl*, a girl young enough to be my age. I leaned forward to get a better view, the girl's eyes scanned the room before meeting mine; we gasped simultaneously.

"*Katie?!*"

"*Christy?!*"

Chapter Twenty-one

My mouth hung open as I stared at her, my mind unable to register the fact that Christy Milano was here, here as in the house of a *Muslim* woman. *What in the world was she doing here?*

Before either of us could get a word in, Habiba remarked, "You two know each other? That's great. This is Christy's first time too, Katie."

We just stood there speechless, Christy looked just as shocked as I did, and I could see from the slight frown on her face that she was trying to imagine all the scenarios that she could that put me here, and I was doing the exact same. *Maybe she's a neighbour. But no, she lives on the other side of London. Maybe her dad's a colleague of Yousuf's. But no, I doubt Yousuf has his own million-pounds worth company and meets Sir Richard Branson for lunch. Maybe they're related somehow. But no, Christy had mentioned more than once the long line of successful British ancestors in her family, on both sides.*

Samra coughed deliberately, breaking the silence, "Habs, how about we go and show Aasiyah the cupcakes you were decorating? She can even help you finish."

"I'd love to," Aasiyah agreed, putting her hand on Christy's arm and saying, "I'll just be in the kitchen," then turning to me and smiling, "It's lovely to see you again, Katie."

"You too," I replied politely.

The three of them left then, closing the kitchen door behind them.

"What are *you* doing here?" I started, just as she exclaimed, "You're *Muslim*!"

We shot each other nervous smiles and then I recalled what she had just said and asked, "How did you know?"

"You look...*different*," she replied, tilting her head to the side, "and you're in Habiba's house."

"So are you."

"Oh no! I...," she flushed red and quickly looked away, "I'm not Muslim."

I furrowed my brow, and then before I could come up with any more bizarre scenarios, I declared, "Let's sit down and talk."

Christy nodded as she seated herself in the sofa opposite me, wringing her hands together and looking extremely on edge. I had never seen Christy like this before and watched her in astonishment. She looked up then, registered the shock on my face, and smiled sheepishly, "You must think I'm a fool for being here."

"Why would I think that?" I asked, before I could stop myself.

"Because I'm not a...," she paused, watching me with apprehension, and then sighed and shut her eyes. She seemed to be thinking hard as she squeezed them tightly for a second, and then suddenly let go. Straightening her back, she turned to face me and opened her eyes, the full force of them hitting me as she stared at me with a sudden ferocity. In a low, tremulous voice she said, "I didn't want this to get out...which is why I've been keeping it a secret. Besides Sarah, *no one knows*," she struggled to control her breathing, the fire in her eyes dying out, as she whispered, "My... my... parents and my brother converted to Islam half a year ago."

I was stunned. *That was not in any of my scenarios.* Not wanting to freak Christy out with my silence, I said, "I don't know what to say. But I can tell you this, if this ever gets out, it'll be from your lips. I promise to not say a word."

"Thank you," she replied sincerely, relief evident in her voice, the worry in her eyes fading, as if a huge load had been taken off her back, "This is actually one of the few Muslim gatherings I've been to. It's hard to watch everything and everyone in your life change so suddenly, and even though I fought it in the beginning, after few months of living with a family that's Muslim, you kind of learn to make compromises. This is one of them, in return my family won't make their conversion public until I'm okay with it. Right now, the thought of telling everyone is just too scary, not that being a Muslim is scary," she added hurriedly in the end.

I smiled at her kindly, "It's okay. I can't say I'd be here if I was in your place. It must have been a very tough choice to come here."

She shook her head, "It's gotten easier over the past few times. I don't exactly fit in, but everyone still welcomes me with open arms," and then looked at me curiously, "I'm dying to know how and why you became Muslim."

I grinned, "My dad. Six months ago. It's kind of the same story as yours. My life was turned upside down, I avoided him completely for a time, and the thought of anyone knowing gave me goosebumps."

Her eyes grew with understanding, "Yeah, exactly. What happened to change it all?"

"I realized I loved him too much to let him go and decided to listen to his side of the story. Once I did, I was pulled in by the truth in Islam, every question I had was answered, and I just couldn't ignore it anymore."

She avoided eye contact carefully and said, "I see. So when did you become Muslim?"

"Yesterday morning actually."

"*Really?* No wonder you were acting so strange during lunch! So are you going to make it public?"

I looked her straight in the eyes as I confided in her, "Part of me wants to and part of me doesn't. It's like...something's holding me back. My fear, I suppose. It's just knowing that once I walk in there with a headscarf on, there's no turning back. But then I'm happy with the way things are going right now. So, who knows? Monday morning, you might just see me parading down the hallway with a Hijab on anyway," I exhaled a half-laugh.

"You're really something, Katie," she gave me a look of wonder, "That's one thing I've always admired about you. You never let anything get in your way."

"You're kidding," I was stunned. Christy Milano in admiration of *me?* What was the world coming to?

"No, I'm serious. I might not have ever shown it before," she declared, "but I've always admired you. You have this inspiring strength inside you and enigmatic nature that just shines out of you and draws other people in."

"Wow, tell that to the butterflies in my stomach." I was touched. Beyond touched. I was amazed.

"And personally, I think Islam suits you, you've got this glow on your face that just…well, suffice it to say, you're going to look even more beautiful in a Hijab."

No way, she did not just say that. Seeing as I'd known Christy since Kindergarten, and up until the last ten minutes was something of a rival of hers, a compliment like that coming from her was unheard of and in its own way that much more special. Wordlessly, I leaned forward and hugged her.

She laughed as I pulled away from her, "Now don't get all emotional on me just yet. I'm waiting for the grand 'Katie reaction' when you meet the other Muslim girls."

"Why? Are they scary?" I asked in alarm.

"Let's just say that you'll probably end up in tears," she joked.

The doorbell rang. Oh, boy.

"So you're telling me you've never tried dates dipped in cream?" Yasmin asked.

"I'm telling you I've never even had a date."

"Oh, really?" Hadiya asked, wagging her eyebrows and causing Christy to burst into laughter.

"*Girl*, you're missing out!" Nahla exclaimed, just as Yasmin said, "Please tell me she's joking."

Sumayah giggled and jumped to her feet, "I'll go fetch some from the kitchen."

"What's the big deal?" I grinned, looking around at them all.

"The big deal is that they're *divine*, and you haven't even tried them," Reemah nudged me with her shoulder.

"All right, all right."

We were sitting in the living room in somewhat of a circle, and the girls who I had met not more than a few hours ago already seemed like sisters to me. Yasmin was Syrian and the youngest of eight siblings, making her the encyclopaedia on marriage and food, and as Hadiya liked to tease, 'our second mother'. Surprisingly, Christy had been right when she said I'd end up in tears, more than once actually, from rolling in laughter at Hadiya's jokes. With a sense of humour that beat even my dad's, and a delightful Australian drawl, I found it hard to keep a straight face when I was around her. Nahla had just moved to London a year ago from Minnesota, and could have been Beyonce's twin if not for her skinny frame and playful green eyes, the mischievous glint in them one of the reasons why she and Hadiya were joined at the hip. Sumayah was the most exotic person I'd met yet, she came from a family of six children, and if I hadn't heard her strong Welsh accent first-hand I wouldn't have believed her father was from there, her Japanese looks being the main downplaying factor. She was a genius, no doubt about it, from the amount of times she'd rattled off quotations of her favourite people in the past few hours, but also had one of the kindest hearts I'd come across so far, her gentle brown eyes looking out for everyone. Reemah just happened to be Habiba's younger sister and if it was possible she was even clumsier, she adored kids to the point that she volunteered to be their 'horsie' for a full half hour, and her mad addiction was anything that began with 'chocolate'.

"Here they are," Sumayah declared, placing a tray of dates and cream onto the carpeted floor.

All eyes looked at me expectantly, and I sighed dramatically, "Okay, here it goes." I picked up a sticky date and after Yasmin's instructions took the seed out, placing it onto the tray, and then dipped it into the cream. I said, "Bismillah", and popped it into my mouth, chewing it slowly as all eyes continued to watch me, and then swallowed it and uttered an astonished, "Unbelievable!"

before reaching for more. Everyone broke out into laughter, teasing me mercilessly and helping themselves to some as well.

Yasmin smirked, "I bet it's as good as the dessert they serve in the school dining hall."

I narrowed my eyes at her, "I still can't believe you guys never once said 'Hello' to me at school."

Reemah laughed, while the others looked at me incredulously, "Like saying 'Hello' to *Katie Anderson* is such an average thing to do. The fact that we're Muslim as well would just make it downright strange. Admit it."

I blushed, "Yeah, you're right. Sorry about that. I'm Muslim now though, so feel free to —"

"Holler your name down the hallway whenever we want?" Hadiya winked.

I grinned, "Something like that. What about Christy? Do you guys say 'Hello' to her?" I tilted my head in Christy's direction.

Christy looked uneasy for a moment before Sumayah shot her a kind smile and remarked, "Nobody in school knows about Christy yet, so we keep our distance."

Yasmin turned to Christy, "Yeah, everyone has a right to their own privacy and personally I think you're taking this all pretty well. You're braver than you think."

In that moment, Christy's eyes met mine, and for the first time ever we understood each other, completely. Her eyes shone with joy as she looked at me and I returned an encouraging smile, conveying to her what my mum had to me. *Don't forget who you are. You're strong.*

Habiba suddenly whipped around the corner, "Girls, come upstairs! The fireworks are starting!"

"*Fireworks?*" we cried simultaneously, stumbling to our feet and following her. She helped the snail-paced toddlers stalling on the staircase, as we waited anxiously at the bottom, and answered us, "Yeah, I told Yousuf to get some fireworks and light them up with the men after the barbecue."

I looked up as Samra suddenly appeared at the top of the stairs for a moment, her shirt ruined after a session of painting with the kids, and hoarsely called for her sons, "Ilyas! Harun! *Quieres ir a ver los fuegos artificiales? Come on!*"

"How are we going to see them from inside?" Christy asked bewilderedly.

Habiba's eyes glinted, "You'll see," and then carrying the last child in her arms ran up the stairs.

We followed her up the staircase and up the next staircase after that to the loft, all the while wondering where everyone was and why all the lights had been turned off. As we emerged into the loft, I couldn't believe my eyes, and blinked a couple of times for good measure. It was huge, but not just huge, it was filled with everyone from the gathering. Mothers held onto their children's hands, bouncing them on their hips, young girls and boys whispered excitedly, nudging each other, their eyes enormous, and surprisingly it was all unbelievably quiet. I looked around me with awe at this wonderful community that had opened up their arms to me and shared their whole world with me, I watched the women joke and laugh together, their heads tilted backwards, I watched the children make space for one another on the tiny chairs they had been given, I watched the girls I had just become friends with sling their arms over each other's shoulders, beckoning me to join them with their enticing grins. And then, when I was safely in the middle of all of this, in between giggling girls and cooing mums, I noticed everyone was looking upwards.

"Katie, look up," Habiba whispered, suddenly behind me. And I did.

The wooden roof of the loft had been replaced by an enormous clear glass surface, and through it I saw a magically lit up sky. Millions of stars winked at me from their glorious faraway abode, red, white, pink, yellow, green blazes of light shot up into the night sky, bursting into dancing flames as they spread out, and the full moon, the shining lamp in the sky looked as magnificent as ever. I ouldn't take my eyes off it, hypnotized by the beauty of the world created by Allah. Staring up at the sky with wonder reminded me of a night not too far back when I had asked an imaginary God for guidance. Tears welled up in my eyes as I realized I had got what I wanted and more.

"It's beautiful, isn't it?" Samra asked, from her position beside me, her daughter Lamya sitting on her shoulders and pointing at the sky.

I searched my mind for a better word to describe the sight before me but couldn't, it was simply beautiful.

Chapter Twenty-two

"I knew you'd love it! What did I tell you, Katie? You had nothing to worry about," my dad gloated, as we drove to the Mosque the following day.

I laughed, "You were completely right."

"Yeah, it's becoming a habit."

"I *can't wait* to see them all again. They're such wonderful people, so sincere and funny and cool," I gushed, my thoughts returning to the previous night.

Just when I thought Habiba couldn't make the night any more spectacular, she brought in hot chocolate and marshmallows. I ended up staying longer than I intended, and when the crowd had returned downstairs, the girls and I lay on a blanket on the floor, laughing the night away. The beauty of it all was how much I had learnt at the same time, they told me stories of the great women in Islam, they explained aspects of Islam to me that only girls could relate to, they told me of their experiences with Hijab, they giggled as they discussed the idea of marriage with me and described their idea of a perfect husband to me. Yasmin promised to teach me a few short chapters of the Quran at the next gathering, while Reemah promised to teach me how to read and write Arabic, Nahla taught me how to wrap a Hijab around my head and Hadiya related some of the parents' convert stories to me in a way that had me holding my stomach with laughter. All in all, it was a night I would never forget, and seemed to even have an effect on Christy, who might not have asked questions every five minutes the way I had, but certainly listened keenly.

"I was worried sick about you half the time," my dad chided me, "but once the fireworks started I knew you were probably having a great time. I mean, you didn't call me right up until eleven!" he ruffled my hair.

We were nearly there, and I eagerly leaned forward in my seat to get a good look at Regents Mosque. I'd worn the light emerald green hijab that Habiba had gifted to me at the end of the night, with a matching full-sleeve shirt and denim skirt that I'd rooted in my wardrobe to find.

"*Allahu Akbar! Allahu Akbar!*" the call to prayer, *Adhaan*, started.

My eyes grew in astonishment as I turned to my dad, "Dad, I know this! I've heard it before!"

He looked at me in surprise, "Really? *When?*"

"At your house, the night after the party. I thought it was some sort of beautiful song," I said, "but....wow, I had no idea *this* was the call to prayer." We were at such a proximity to the Mosque now that we could hear the Adhaan being called out, and I revelled in its beauty.

"You must have heard my prayer alarm ringing," he spoke with recognition, "I've set the Adhaan to play at each prayer time." He chuckled as he glanced at me, "Every time you discover something new about Islam your eyes light up like they did when you were younger and unwrapping your Christmas presents."

I beamed, "This is much better than any present I've ever gotten, to be honest."

He nodded in an 'I-know-what-you-mean' way and then we continued to listen to the rest of the Adhaan in silence. As my dad parked the car, I held my mobile in anticipation, remembering the promise the girls had made yesterday to welcome me to the mosque when I arrived. Within seconds it rang and I answered it, listening to Yasmin's instructions as she directed me to where they were sitting in the women's praying area. Saying a quick goodbye to my dad once we had reached the women's entrance, I entered the mosque timidly, gaping at how huge it was. Taking advantage of the fact that there wasn't much of a crowd on a weekday, I happily took in my surroundings as I calmly made my way to where the girls were sitting in a circle, grinning all over my face.

I crouched down and laid my hands on Reemah's eyes as I winked at the rest of the girls. I could feel her smile as she said, "*Anybody* but Katie Anderson," making me laugh as I let go of her.

"Assalamu alaikum wa rahmatullahi wa barakaatuhu," I said, as she turned her head to smile at me cheekily.

Yasmin's face lit up as she exclaimed, "You're a quick learner, MashaAllah," and then pulled me in for a hug.

230

The rest of the girls got up from the circle they had been sitting in and joined her to welcome me.

"So what do you think of the *Masjid*?" Sumayah asked, using the Arabic term for mosque, and gesturing around her.

"It's absolutely beautiful," I replied, loving the sense of peace and serenity I'd felt once I'd entered, "It feels like home."

Nahla's eyes twinkled at me, "This place is home for me too. I can't remember a single time when I didn't come here for the Friday prayer."

"You mean ever since you moved here, right? Around a year ago," Hadiya teased.

"In matters like this, time is really not of the essence," she countered with a smile.

"You know, that hijab really suits you, MashaAllah," Sumayah remarked, bringing the attention back to me.

"Oh. Thanks. I mean, uh JazakAllahu Khair," I replied self-consciously, immediately raising a hand to adjust my hair, as was my habit, only to find myself patting my hijab awkwardly.

Yasmin smiled kindly, "It's okay, it's normal to forget, and it takes time to get used to the Arabic words."

Hadiya grinned, "I was hopeless when I was a child, after my parents reverted. Remember?" she nudged Sumayah, "And Sumayah, here, was the one to correct me every time."

"How could I not remember?" Sumayah's mouth twitched,

"You were always mixing up your 'MashaAllah' and 'JazakAllah'. I remember the first time I witnessed it for myself, when you won the Muslim Children Creativity award at an event, and once they presented the gift to you on the stage, instead of replying with 'JazakAllah', you kept gushing, 'MashaAllah, MashaAllah' to the presenter, as if you were *praising* him instead of thanking him! Poor guy, he looked so awkward standing there, not knowing what to say."

Her story left us all in hysterics and when I was finally able to catch my breath, I said, "I can imagine. I mean, everything's so new when you've just reverted, like there's this world out there that you never thought even existed, for you to explore."

"Exactly," Hadiyah nodded her head, "It's exciting but can be a little overwhelming at the same time. Unless, you've got some supportive friends to back you up," she looked at the rest of the girls, a mixture of gratitude and gratefulness shining in her eyes.

Yasmin returned the smile and then turned to me, "So, Katie, will you be wearing it tomorrow to school?" she asked curiously, bringing us back to the topic of my hijab.

I looked down, fingering it, "Well, yes, I'm planning to. I just...I don't know if I can do it. What if I chicken out just before entering school and remove it? I'm not sure if I have it in me—"

"Hey," Sumayah squeezed my hands, looking at me until I returned her gaze, "you'll be *fine*, okay? Don't worry about it. Every one of us has been blessed with inner strength, and it shines out most when we do that which we believe in, when we have a reason to stand up and face a crowd, when we come to the amazing realization that we can do *anything* we truly put our minds to."

I smiled at her graciously, my mum's words echoing in my head once more, *Don't forget who you are.* "You're right, you're absolutely right."

"Yeah, it's not every day Katie Anderson walks into school with a *hijab* on," Nahla whistled.

"Nahla!" they all cried, as I chuckled, "It's fine. I was thinking the exact same thing anyway. And I have to face the fact that people will stare, but it's up to me to change their looks from shock and surprise into respect and awe."

"Spoken profoundly by a true Muslim," Hadiyah grinned, "Well, just know that we'll all be there looking out for you, we'll be your support system, InshaAllah. And you'll have Allah on your side, so everything will go just perfectly."

"JazakAllahu Khair," I replied sincerely.

We continued to chat for a few minutes as the topic shifted to prayer, and they explained to me the way Muslims pray in congregation and the higher level of reward gained for that, the direction Muslims faced when praying, and that another, shorter version of the call to prayer, the *Iqama*, would be called to signal the beginning of the prayer. Just then, the Iqama sounded and we all got up, stood side by side in a line facing the Qibla, the direction that Muslims face when praying, and the prayer started. The recitation of the Quran was extraordinary, it was everything I'd imagined and better, filling me with a feeling of peace, hope and fear all at once. The moment I touched my forehead to the ground was when I actually realized that I was crying, tears of gratefulness flowed down my face as the unique beauty of the position I was in hit me, as the blessing of being Muslim enveloped me.

Once we had finished praying, we walked arm in arm towards the mosque's exit, the girls listening while I raved on about the strong rhythmic words of the Quran and the Imam's melodious tune. We reached the door, and emerged to the loud honking sound of the cars around us, moving slowly in and out of the parking lot. They walked me over to my car, and I cupped my hands over my eyes against the glaring sunlight, in search of my dad, when suddenly my phone buzzed in my pocket. I picked it up and read the message he'd sent me, 'Be there in 5. Just greeting some friends.'

I turned to the girls, "Again, thank you so much for coming! It was great having you all here with me, nothing more than wonderful," I smiled inwardly, "I seem to be using that word a lot lately. So, I'll see you all tomorrow at school then?"

They nodded as Reemah jokingly remarked, "We'll be the ones with Hijabs on."

I laughed, hugging each of them goodbye, and then sat in the car as I waited for my dad. I looked around at the people coming out of the mosque, so many different sizes and colours, races and nationalities, and all united by one similar belief, the truth, *Islam.* There weren't as many women as men, since praying in the mosque was only obligatory on every male, however, women were encouraged to pray in the mosque on Fridays. Just then, I spotted my dad walking out of the mosque, laughing as he talked to a friend. I briefly glanced at his friend and then my eyes were dragged back to his face as I stared in amazement. *Was I imagining him?* I rubbed my eyes and looked again, *It is him! But...how?*

My phone vibrated suddenly, snapping me out of my reverie, and I quickly retrieved it out of my pocket again, "Hel—"

"*Katie! Where have you been?* I've been trying to call you for the past hour!" Jayne yelled in a high-pitched voice.

"Sorry," I pulled the phone slightly away from my ear, "I put my phone on silent because I was praying at the Mosque. What happened? Is something wrong?"

"You wouldn't believe it," she managed to say instead of her usual bursting with the information.

"Jayne, try me," I said, looking up at my dad's friend again. Nothing could be more unbelievable than what I was looking at right now.

"So, I'm sitting in the kitchen, eating some Ben and Jerry's ice cream, when in walks Jeff all dressed up. I asked him where he was going and *guess* what he said?!"

"The mosque."

"Yeah, and I asked him why and....wait, *what? How did you know?*" she asked with irritation, realizing that the major surprise which she'd just spent an entire hour waiting to tell me hadn't been one.

"Because I'm looking at him right now, he's talking to Dad. What's he doing here?"

"Isn't it obvious?" she laughed, her excitement reignited, "he went to the mosque to become Muslim."

Chapter Twenty-three

"See you tomorrow, Dad. Assalam u alaikum," I waved goodbye to him as I stood by the front door, half an hour later. I stepped inside and closed the door, placing my rucksack on the floor and then began to untie my shoes. "I'm home," I yelled, announcing myself to whoever was there, before making my way to the living room and picking up the newspaper. Five minutes later, and with no reply, I padded softly into room after room downstairs searching for Mark and mum, and then ran upstairs, now thoroughly confused. "Mark! Where are you? *Mum?*"

I entered my room in a rush, thinking that this would be the last place I'd find them but instead stumbled upon the sight of my mum sleeping soundly on my bed. Stepping forward quietly, I noticed how her head lay flat on the bed and her hands tucked tightly around my pillow as if she never wanted to let go, and in that moment she looked so vulnerable that I wished I hadn't left her for the weekend. Picking up the latest novel I'd been reading from my side table, I sat on the white comforter in my room, tucked my legs under me, and waited for my mum to wake up.

Forty minutes later my mum opened her eyes, yawning noisily

and pulling herself upright. She stretched her arms over her head, arching her back as she fully woke up then suddenly noticed me in the corner and exclaimed, "Katie, you're back!"

I smiled, "Yeah, I've been back a while."

She checked her watch, "Oh. Sorry, I didn't mean to fall asleep. I was just..," she frowned, as if trying to recall how exactly she'd ended up asleep on my bed, "in your room because..."

"Because you missed me so much you needed a reminder of me?" I asked cheekily.

Instead of the snappy comeback I was expecting, her body seemed to still and a look of shock flitted past her face, and then jumping to her feet, she replied breezily, "I'll just use the bathroom and then you can tell me about your weekend. Did you eat lunch?"

"Yeah."

"Good."

As she left the room, my eyebrows drew together as I wondered about her earlier reaction to my joke. My accepting Islam had undoubtedly affected her, even as she tried to cover it up. The question now was *how deeply had it?*

A few minutes later, she entered my room again, her face fresh and in her hands a shopping bag. "Katie. I need to talk to you."

I raised my head to look at her nervous face, my eyes darting to each of her eyes as I pleaded, "Mum, I know that this has hurt you, my reversion, and I—"

"No, no. Katie I..." she paused, glancing away and then brought her eyes back to mine, now glittering with tears. "I want to speak first."

A lump filled my throat as I watched her and moved my head a few fractions in a nod.

She led me to the bed so we could sit down, and said, "There's so much I want to say, but I think I'll start off by telling you a story, a story about my past that I've never told anyone else," her eyes took on a reflective sheen as she continued, "It all happened around a year before me and your dad divorced. When your grandmother died that year, I was distraught and depressed for months, your dad thought it was mainly because of her death, but it wasn't. It was mainly because I couldn't understand why? Why we had to die? Why we had to leave our children, our husbands, our *families* and stay in a grave forever?"

I laid a hand on her shoulder to calm her down and she exhaled heavily, dropping her head, "I wanted to know my purpose for living but everywhere I looked, everything I read made me more confused. Why were we being told to worship a man? A man, a person with faults like anyone else, an *imperfect* person. I wondered where everything came from and when I studied scientology and different theories, they just sounded like such a load of rubbish to me, the idea that this entire world came about by chance," she clicked her fingers, raising her head suddenly.

"No, I knew for a fact that hearts weren't beating by chance, minds weren't thinking by chance and people weren't *dying by chance*. I decided for myself that there was a God, but what ate at me for months, seeping into every corner of my life, was one simple question, what was my *purpose*?" she asked, turning towards me and staring intensely into my eyes, as if the question was being posed to me.

I held her gaze until she finally looked away, "Your dad was amazing though, he gave me space, he went around buying me pamphlets of every religion I asked, he reassured me time and time again that it was just a phase I was going through, but after a year of being a mother and father to you kids, after a year of watching me laugh one moment and then stop and wonder why I was enjoying life the next, it became too hard for him. He begged me to go to a psychiatrist with him but I refused, I told him I'd only go if they could answer my one, simple question," she chuckled dryly.

"In the end, he couldn't do anything but leave me, I watched his heart breaking apart and I told him to go. I can't tell you how much your dad has done for me, he loved you and Mark so much that he promised to be there for you always, and he left me only when there was no hope left, no light left in me, nothing left for him to do anymore, and even then, it was I who asked him to go," her eyes welled up with tears and she wiped them away hastily.

"One of my biggest regrets in life is hurting your dad like that, ruining a perfect marriage, but you know, Katie, it was the divorce that also brought me back. Suddenly I had to be a mother to you and Mark again, take responsibility, put others' lives before mine so I decided I'd live life as long as I was still in this world, and eventually with the help of you guys I started to enjoy life again. I never knew what I'd tell you about religion, I mean, on one hand I believed in God but on the other hand, I had no idea why we were here. So I let you both believe I was Christian, because everyone around you was, your dad was, your friends were, why complicate things for you? And slowly I stopped thinking about it, I let the matter rest until well, *this* happened," she closed her eyes for a moment as if in pain. Watching her, I realized that all my perceptions about her so far had been completely wrong. The mum that I'd imagined had led a simple, easy life with no worries had in fact experienced more turmoil in her life during those few years than I could possibly imagine.

"In all my life," she stammered, her emotions filling her voice, "there's always been one thing that I've been proud of...being a *mother*. But for the first time, I've done something no mother ever should, an unforgivable act," her voice broke and her lips trembled as she continued, "by judging my daughter by the mistakes that *I* made." Tears streamed down her face, but before I could get a word in, she held her hand up, "Let me finish. Katie, I'm so far from perfect that at times I wonder if I should even be raising two kids. But...but I promised myself that whatever happens I would take care of them and *never* let them go through what I did, I would give them *everything*, answers for everything, even... even if I had to resort to lying, but I wouldn't let them question their lives. And then...," she was talking between sobs now, roughly wiping tears from her face, "in the past few weeks since Jack returned, I started seeing all these signs of my past in you. You looked so worried and anxious, acting the way I had during that episode in my life, and it *scared me*."

She stood up, pacing back and forth, "I couldn't sleep at night, I couldn't think about anything but you and that...certain emptiness in your eyes. It was like a bad dream that I couldn't wake up from. And when you came back from the party, that was it! You had totally changed, you roamed around the house deep in your thoughts, you mumbled things without thinking, you stopped talking to *Jeff*," she looked at me incredulously, "anyone who knows you would know that that meant something was wrong."

"And, God, Katie you didn't make it easy, you shut yourself up so *tightly*...it was probably the most frightening thing that had ever happened to me. But I knew I had to keep trying, I had to get you to talk to me, and when you finally did, what did you say? *That you were interested in Islam,"* she said, with the same astonished voice that she had used before, *"*and then everything just came crumbling down at once. I was sure that...that I had to have done things in life that made you like this, like *me*."

She focused her gaze on the floor, "That night when I told you I was going out, I went to see Mark in his dorm room. I needed to know something was still stable in my life, that he wasn't like me too, and," she smiled through her tears "God, you just gotta love that kid. He said, *'Mum, I love you and I'm like you in a hundred ways, and I want to be like you for the rest of my life but you should know one thing about me by now; when it comes to matters of life and God and questions, I'm clueless and I'm gonna stay clueless, because I'm happy this way. Life's easy,'* and those words are what put me back together, knowing that I hadn't done such a bad job. But when you declared that you were Muslim the very next day, it was such a shock, such a major shock and I just kept thinking to myself, 'You've failed, Ellie. Look what you've done to Katie,' and then I'd look at your face and think, 'Why is she *smiling* like that? I never smiled like that', and there were all these conflicting emotions, and I just had to tell you to never forget who you are, because that was what I was frightened about most," she came forward and held my hands in hers.

"When you left for the weekend, I couldn't get your smile out of my head and when I talked to Mark again he told me about the conversation he'd had with you in the car, it explained so much, and he went on to say that he'd also seen a change in you, but he called it a *beautiful* change, and the more I thought about it the more I realized that I was complicating things and that one thing was certain. You, Katie, are stronger than me, you always have and always will be and that's why you weren't dragged down like I was. Instead, you found what you were looking for, you found solace in a religion. After that, I just couldn't wait to see you and tell you that," she touched my face gently, "I'm so proud of you, so *very* proud of you. You're Muslim, and I love you and I hope that you will forgive me."

"Mum," I cried, throwing my arms around her, my face lined with tears, "I love you." I'd never heard anything more heart-wrenching, and my emotions were all over the place as I clung on to her, not wanting to let go. She rubbed my back, her sweet voice soothing me until my cries subsided and I pulled back to look at her, "You're wrong, Mum, there was nothing unforgivable about this, it was natural. It was what anyone in your place would have done, but you, you did even more than that, you conquered it, Mum, you accepted me after all that and didn't try to change me. *You conquered it.*"

Her eyes grew as I spoke, a look of immense relief taking over her face as realization hit her, "I did, I really did, and it's about time."

I looked at my mother with new eyes, understanding that she had been through something tough, had wondered and asked questions like I did, had braced the storm until it had become too much for her. My dad was greater in my eyes now too, the fact that he'd supported her, taken care of her, and loved her throughout it all, filled me with awe at his patience. I wanted to tell my mum that the journey I'd taken didn't just give me solace, it taught me that the purpose of this life was to prepare me for the next journey, the next chapter, the next life, but after hearing a story that turned her life upside down I decided to give it some time, to show her through my actions, to do exactly what my dad had said, *to be a Muslim.*

"That was an incredible story, I don't even know what to say, but I'm glad that everything worked out in the end. And I'm happy too, Mum," I beamed, "I've only been Muslim for two days but I love it and every time I think about it, I get this thrill, and I can't wait to learn more."

"I know, I can see it on your face," she smiled, "You're glowing. So, tell me about your weekend. How did it go?"

"Oh, it was great! On Friday, Dad taught me more about Islam and we ordered Thai and then on Saturday we went to his friend's house for a Muslim party."

She raised her eyebrows, "Interesting. I can just imagine how nervous you must have been, how did it go?"

I laughed, "I was nervous, but it turned out to be fantastic! I met all sorts of people from different countries; Palestine, Pakistan, Korea, Germany, Australia, Japan! And I made friends, five incredible girls, and we talked about everything, school, boys, life. And you know, the one thing that really worried me was starting hijab, but when they told me about their experiences with hijab and encouraged me I realized that, in the end, it's all worth it. And I'm going to start tomorrow."

"That's good, just always keep in mind that when you believe in something and stand by it, you're on top of the world, and you can do *anything*. And about that hijab," her eyes were shining as she handed me the shopping bag, "I went shopping in the morning and got you a little something,"

I looked at the bag curiously, and then at her, "Noooo, you didn't!"

243

"Open it."

I opened the shopping bag and reached inside, already knowing what I was going to find, as my fingers caught hold of a soft cloth and gently pulled it out. It was blue, but not just any blue, deep sky blue like my eyes. I looked up at her in amazement, knowing that it must have taken ages to find.

"Try it on," she said softly.

I stood up and walked up to my mirror, seeing myself differently for the first time in days, the same mirror that I had used to make sure my hair looked voluminous enough, my legs looked long enough, and I looked good enough to prance around London, now reflected the image of a girl covered up, her hands cradling a blue cloth, her eyes staring wondrously at herself. Not taking my eyes off my reflection, I put the hijab on the way I had been taught, wrapping it around my head and then pinning it tightly. Tears flooded my eyes, as I continued to stare at myself, blurring the image in front of me and when I blinked to clear my view, I saw a figure standing beside me. My mother's hands touched my shoulders, and with a smile as bright as the morning sky, she said, "Katie, darling, you look like a princess."

Chapter Twenty-four

"You know the funny thing is," my mum said, in between mouthfuls of Frosties, "I had never even considered Islam as a religion people were converting to until your dad did, I really had no idea. And when he told me that he had, I said, "You gotta be kidding me". It just didn't seem real. But now, after always being told Islam is an oppressive religion, I've noticed for myself that you've both changed for the better. It just goes to show how much the media has an effect on us."

"Mhmm," I mumbled, munching on my own bowl of Nesquick.

It was the following morning and I was sitting at the kitchen table having breakfast with mum and buttoning up the long-sleeved turquoise cotton shirt I had chosen to wear with jeans to school. My hands trembled at just the thought of revealing my true self to everyone, excitement filling me even as I felt fluttering butterflies in my stomach at the thought of actually doing it.

"And now, surprisingly, I've actually started noticing Muslims more when I go outside. I see them at Tesco, at Primark, at

Harrods, in the parking lot, everywhere. I had no idea there were so many Muslims in London!"

"I know, right? They're everywhere," Mark chuckled, coming up from behind me and ruffling my hair. He'd hurried back home last night after realizing he'd forgotten some things, and after seeing us both in such a happy mood, our mouths filled with Baskin Robbins ice cream, our eyes on the Tom and Jerry reruns we were watching, he decided to stay and join in. I'd acted as surprised as I could when he told me his news of Oxford, my mouth forming a big O, but I guess it must have been the incessant giggling that followed that gave me away.

I smirked, "You'd be surprised. Oh, and that reminds me, guess who I saw at the party? You wouldn't believe it."

"Who?" they asked simultaneously.

"Christy," I grinned as both of their eyes popped out, "No, I'm not joking. Her family became Muslim half a year ago, and that was the reason for her being there, she's accepted them. I was on the phone with her yesterday and she said it was all right to tell you guys, but up till now it's all been pretty hushed so don't say anything."

My mum opened her mouth and then closed it, and then opened it again, "*Sandra Milano became Muslim*. Wow, I would never have guessed! I mean, I haven't seen her for quite some time but...that's amazing."

"Yeah, she's changed her name to Aasiyah now."

"Everyone keeps surprising me," my mum exclaimed, "next you're gonna tell me Jayne and Jeff became Muslim."

Fighting back a smile, I nodded my head, and after seeing her jaw drop open, burst into laughter. "Not Jayne, but Jeff did. I found out yesterday, we were at the mosque and I saw him come out with Dad. I was sure I was seeing things, but then Jayne called and confirmed the news."

"She's making it up," Mark shook his head.

"Don't mess with me, Katie. That's too good to be true," she said, looking at me crossly.

I made a face, "Would I lie to you? And why would it be too good to be true?"

"Because it's obvious you both like each other and now that he's Muslim you can get married and have gorgeous kids and grandkids—" her grin grew as she spoke.

"Mum!" my cheeks went a funny shade of red as Mark roared with laughter.

She laughed, "Just dreaming here, kiddo, give me some hope."

"I can't believe you think that," I said in amazement, and then when Mark turned to fetch a bottle of milk out of the fridge, leaned in and whispered to my mum confidentially, "I mean, I'm not that obvious, am I?"

"Tell that to your tomato red skin," she whispered back, just as Mark whipped around again. She winked at me in a completely indiscreet way as she asked, "But really, he became Muslim? How?"

The blush on my cheeks increased as Mark raised an eyebrow, "Well, Jayne said he'd actually known about Islam before I did and was interested in it. Christy's brother, Lionel, and Jeff have always been close and when Lionel converted to Islam he began to preach it to Jeff at their weekly basketball games. And then, Dad came back with his news and well, I was pretty furious in the beginning, and Jayne said she thought that actually made him interested in Islam, he wanted to know why people hated it, especially me, since...we're close."

"We know," my mum interjected, winking.

I rolled my eyes, with a blush. "So, anyway, he even confronted me about it once at school, which made me think about it some more as well, and I guess, led me to accept it. Jayne said the fact that he had most of his questions answered and that two of the people he deeply respects, Lionel and Dad, had converted, motivated him to accept Islam as well. But that he really just needed one last push, and um...she said that after I talked to him about Islam in the parking lot the other day, I guess I said something that had made sense to him, because he came home completely changed. And that was it. I was the last piece in the puzzle."

"How beautiful," Mark quipped, wiping away non-existent tears from his eyes, and then jumping away from my outstretched arm.

"Well, if a story like that doesn't bring one to tears, I don't know what does," my mum said, smiling right at me, "So is Jack picking you up? Because if he is, you have exactly ten minutes to get ready."

"Oh, great," I said, jumping up and dashing up the stairs to get ready. After brushing my teeth in record time, I went to my room and searched around for anything I might need, picked up a du'aa book and my mobile, stuffed them in my bag, and then went to the mirror to put my hijab on. I wrapped it around my head carefully, and stepped back to look at myself properly. The hijab brought out the colour of my eyes magnificently, as if it had been made just for me, and the jeans and shirt I'd chosen enhanced the colour, making me look a vivid blue. *I'm a Muslim*, I said to myself, the thrill of it filling every inch of me as I grinned, not bad.

Not bad at all.

"*Hasbi Allahu wa ni'mal wakeel*," my dad said, his body turned towards me in the car as we sat in the empty school parking lot.

I repeated after him, my heart in my throat, every inch of me tingling with an unexplainable anxiety that had enveloped me all of a sudden during the car ride here. I checked my phone for the third time, "Come on, Jayne. *Pick* up. Oh God, she's supposed to be here. Dad, I don't know if I can do this!"

"Yes, you can," he looked into my eyes and held my shoulders. "You've got absolutely nothing to worry about. It'll be a breeze for you. You're Katie Anderson after all," he smiled crookedly.

249

"And I inherited the Anderson genes of confidence. Yada yada yada," I grinned.

His eyes twinkled, "But not just that. You've got the added bonus of having," he pointed upwards, "Him on your side."

I jumped up as all of a sudden someone rapped sharply on the car door behind me. I whipped around to find myself looking at none other than Jayne. I opened the window, "*Where were you? I kept trying to call you!*"

"Sorry, I was busy shopping. Come on, get out of the car, I'll show you."

"*Shopping?*" I gave her a 'you've-gone-utterly-berserk' look. "Oh my god, this better be worth it," I muttered, stepping out of the car and looking around consciously, "but really nothing could be worth making your best friend wait anxiously...wha... *what are you wearing?*"

She grinned at me, as I stared at the baggy jeans and long, oversized shirt she was sporting. "I thought that since I couldn't wear a hijab, I'd wear these instead. Now, I'm wearing decent clothes that are strange enough to distract attention from you, not that you'll need distracting attention from because you look gorgeous as usual but you know, I wanted to support you somehow and wearing a miniskirt would have just—" she rambled on as I suddenly grabbed her and pulled her into a bear hug.

"I can't believe you did this for me. Jayne Collins, once again you have succeeded in surprising me, *to the core*," I couldn't help laughing. *Allah's making everything easier.*

My dad honked the horn, and I told Jayne to wait a minute

as I leaned in to look at him, "Sorry, I got carried away for a moment, forgot you were there. So, I'll remember that du'aa you told me and say it every time I'm nervous, which would basically mean every minute of the day and—"

"How about I tell you something that'll take your mind off it?" he asked.

I gave him a bemused look, "Okay."

"I've finally chosen a Muslim name for myself."

"*Really?* Spill!"

He grinned, "Yahya."

"Yahya," I repeated, liking the sound of it, "It's beautiful, Dad," I smiled warmly, "What does it mean?"

"It means "will live" and it was a name that Allah chose for a Prophet's son that no man had ever had before. I liked it and thought it was unique."

"It is, and it suits you. And you have sort of taken my mind off it, because now I can't stop thinking about deciding on a name too," I grinned, and then saying goodbye to him, closed the door and turned to Jayne.

"You know, I don't get it, even in that you manage to look like you could be a runway model," I said to her, as she slung her arm around my neck and we began to walk towards the school.

"Hmm...really? You think I have a shot at it?"

"Are you kidding me?" I asked, "but I'd rather you didn't. Personally, I feel sorry for models. They live on money they earn by showing off their bodies, they have to work out constantly to stay thin, and they can't even eat great food!"

Jayne laughed, "Well, then, you should be glad to know that fortunately *this* friend of yours totally agrees with you. I mean, can you imagine life without Ben and Jerry's once a week? Or those Lindor chocolates we get from..." I listened to her rant on about food as we entered school, and when dozens of people turned to look at me and gape, I listened to her rant on about how rude it was to stare, and when I entered Maths class to have my teacher scowl at me and then drop his books on his toe, I listened to her rant on about how 'what goes around comes around', and when Muslim girls began to smile at me shyly, I listened to her rant on about how lovely it felt to be appreciated by others, but mostly when everything seemed like it might be too hard and people stopped to stare, I listened to her rant on about how easy I made it look to be gorgeous, look gorgeous and most of all, feel gorgeous.

Chapter Twenty-five

Hasbi Allahu Wa Ni'mal Wakeel. Hasbi Allahu Wa Ni'mal Wakeel. Hasbi Allahu Wa Ni'mal Wakeel.

Allah (Alone) is Sufficient for me, and He is the Best Trustee of affairs...

I repeated in my head like a mantra as I neared the door that opened up to the dining hall. Taking a deep breath, I pushed open the door and walked in, with Jayne by my side. I noticed the difference instantaneously, moving mouths stopped, the sound of laughter died in the air, heads turned swiftly, and then all eyes were on me. *I'm a Muslim. I'm a Muslim. I'm a Muslim!* I lifted my head an inch higher, straightened my shoulders, and walked forward with an air of confidence. I knew that in that instant when every eye would be watching my every move, every whisper would be related to my every move, and every thought would be judging my every move, I had to make a good impression and let everyone know that this is who I was now. Without thinking twice about it, I walked toward my usual table where Christy and her friends were already seated.

Jayne grinned, whispering, "This is so much fun. Everyone keeps giving me these odd looks, it makes me want to stick my tongue out and do something totally bizarre."

I fought back a smile, whispering back, "It's probably because they just can't understand the fact that you look great in everything you wear."

We reached the table and moved to sit down when a voice cut us short, "*What* do you think you're doing?"

I brought my eyes up to Eva's, looked at her evenly, and said, "It's quite obvious, I'm sitting down."

"*No*, you're not. We don't mix with people like *you*," Eva sneered.

"I hope that includes me then," Jayne said, stepping away from the table, "because I couldn't stand sitting at a table with *you*. God knows why I put up with it for this long."

Eva looked shocked momentarily as an audible gasp circulated the hall, before skimming her eyes over Jayne's outfit and saying, "Well, fortunately, the *under-privileged* are excluded as well."

"Oh yeah, there's nothing that screams under-privileged louder than an Armani exchange shirt and Roberto Cavalli jeans."

A couple of chuckles went round as Eva's mouth fell open, but before she could get a word in, I asked, "And what are people like me like?"

I wanted to give her the benefit of the doubt, to ignore the look of intense disgust she shot me, and to find out why there was such a sudden change in her behaviour towards me. But the words that came out of her mouth next ruled everything out. "Terrorists.

Islamic terrorists. "

"Nice label. It's funny though, the girl sitting beside you happens to be just like me," I countered.

Christy, who had been staring at the table all along, snapped her head up and shot me a look mixed with confusion and betrayal.

Eva, however, turned her head to the other side, to the girl who I had directed my statement to and said, "She's different, she's like us."

Sarah, having kept quiet during the exchange, now stared icily at Eva, "Actually, I'm not," and then stood up and aligned herself beside me, "I'm just like her."

Eva narrowed her eyes, "Well, what would Zack say to that?"

Sarah shrugged indifferently, "If you get a chance to ask him, let me know. We're over."

Eva stared at her in complete astonishment and then turned to me with a sneer, "What's wrong with you Muslims? Always obeying and following others."

"You've got it wrong, we obey no one but God and we follow His messengers. We have a purpose for living, a reason for being here, and just for living that way, Muslims are treated badly," I said, standing my ground.

"Are you kidding me? Muslims kill innocent people all the time. It's all over the TV. You'd be blind not to notice. And now you're just like them, Katie Anderson. You're no better than a murderer," she leered, staring daggers at me.

There was pin drop silence as everyone waited for my reaction and I calculatedly thought about what to say. I felt a mixture of anger, betrayal, hurt, but mostly, sympathy. Sympathy at the realization that people actually believed that, and about Islam no less, a word that literally meant *Peace* and a religion that called to that. But I also knew that there would be no point in me slashing back at people like Eva with words, I would just have to make them understand.

"Eva, I really don't mean to sound harsh when I say this, but do you ever look around and see the world rather than watch it on TV or read about it in a magazine? Because there is a world out there, with people like me, who convert to Islam every day, who leave all the glamour, all the ease of life, and all the problems in their heart," I spoke kindly but firmly, knowing that more than two hundred students were hanging on my every word, "And I seriously doubt they do that to become part of a religion that 'wages war against people'. Islam is nothing like that, *there is no terrorism involved*, we don't sign up for it like soldiers, we embrace it as people who have finally discovered the truth. Believe it or not, but I've never been happier than I am right now. I'm Muslim and I'm free. No more social expectations, no more living a life with no meaning, no more pretending to be someone I'm not. Like it or not, but this is who I am. "

Before Eva was able to even retort, Jayne stepped forward from her place beside me, "My best friend's a Muslim, my brother's a Muslim, I *love* Muslims. Like it or not, but this is who I am."

All eyes turned in shock to Jeff, who had been listening intently from his spot with the football team. With determined eyes, he too stood up, the centre of everyone's attention now. And then the captain of the football team and every students' role model, declared loudly, "I'm a Muslim and proud to be. Like it or not, but this is who I am."

Mouths fell open, and eyes popped out of their sockets at his announcement, and even more so when the football teams' favourite midfielder stood up, walked over to Jeff and said, "I'm the vice-captain of the football team and I'd be nothing without this guy over here. Like it or not, but this is who I am." One by one, each member of the football team stood up loyally, backed up Jeff and repeated the statement, "*Like it or not, but this is who I am.*"

"I'm the worst cook ever, I hate it when people assume everyday stuff can't be done in a wheelchair, I absolutely love Katie Anderson. Like it or not, but this is who I am," Sophie grinned, appearing out of nowhere and suddenly right beside me.

"I hate modelling and I'm quitting. I'm a Muslim and I'm going to start acting like one. Like it or not, but this is who I am," Sarah smiled, looking relieved.

"I'm a Muslim, Islam is my life. Like it or not, but this is who I am," Yasmin said, standing up from across the hall, each of her friends following her.

"I can speak five languages fluently but have a record for the worst spelling. I'm a Muslim. Like it or not, but this is who I am," Nahla said.

"I'm possibly the most klutzy person in London. I'm Muslim and I love everything about being one. Like it or not, but this is who I am," Reemah shot me a smile.

"I can't tell the difference between a crocodile and an alligator, even though I'm Australian. I'm a Muslim; I can't imagine life without Islam. Like it or not, but this is who I am," Hadiya grinned from ear to ear.

"I have a habit of making up stories about where I'm from because no one can ever tell. I'm a Muslim. Like it or not, but this is who I am," Sumayah said, grinning like a Cheshire cat.

"I hate being commanded by others and believe in justice and that everybody should be treated equally. Like it or not, but this is who I am," Megan surprised me by standing up and smiling coldly at a stunned Eva.

"I can't stand it when people who are exceptionally talented are labelled 'geeks'. Like it or not, but this is who I am," a red-haired boy stood up.

"I hate conformity, full stop. Like it or not, but this is who I am," a girl stood up, from the opposite side of the hall.

My head swivelled around at each person's statement, my eyes shone with exhilarating happiness as people continued to stand up, my mind filled with one thought, *Without the help of Allah, I couldn't have done this. Allahu Akbar! Allah is the Greatest!*

I finally looked back at Eva, when over forty people were standing by my cause, to see her lips trembling and her hands shaking. "Well, I...I don't care. You're all crazy. Right, Christy? They're all crazy, aren't they?"

Christy's eyes were filled with tears as she stared at the standing crowd around her, and she got up, moved away from the table as Eva looked on with bewilderment, and came to stand in front of me. Looking me straight in the eye, with an indescribable look of sincerity, she said, "Crazy? No, far from it. Amazing? Definitely," and then turning around to face Eva, said, "My family is Muslim, my friends are Muslims, I *love* being with Muslims. Like it or not, but this is who I am."

Eva was speechless as she stared blankly at Christy, her eyes mirroring her feelings, as she watched her status in school crumble into pieces. Then shrieking angrily, she hauled her bag up and marched out the door.

I turned to Christy, "Wow. I can't believe you did that."

"Me neither," she said, astounded, "Wait...I can't believe *you* did that! That was incredible!"

I turned to look at Jayne, Sophie and Sarah, and then my gaze swept across the room, looking at all the people who had stood by me, watching them as they laughed and mixed freely with one another, no more groups dividing them. My eyes glittered with tears as I noticed the football mid-fielder slap his hand on the red-haired boy's back in a friendly gesture, as the rest of the football team surrounded Jeff and cheered his name, as a smiling cheerleader walked up to the girls from the Math club and invited them for a shopping trip, as students intrigued about Islam went up and asked my Muslim friends questions, and as Megan linked arms with the girl who had spoken against conformity. I had never witnessed anything as beautiful as the sight before me, and I knew then that Islam was the best thing that had ever happened to me; Islam united hearts and inspired people.

I smiled enigmatically at my friends, "I wasn't alone. God was with me, everyone in this dining hall was with me. I can't thank you all enough."

"Well," Jayne half-smiled, "it would be really helpful if you could cause a distraction of some sort, and in the process extend the break timing, because I'm *starving*."

We all laughed, and I winked at her, "I have something better in mind."

Whipping out my mobile, I called my dad, as Jayne looked on suspiciously.

"Hey, honey, I was just about to call you. How'd it go?"

"God, dad, it was terrific! I'll tell you *everything* later, I don't have much time. Lunch break's nearly over and I kind of need a favour."

I could hear the smile in his voice, "Your wish is my command."

"You remember when you told me Principal Watson asked to have his newest mansion designed by you? Well, could you somehow get him to extend our break timing? Nobody's actually eaten yet."

"Better yet, I'll get him to give you all the day off."

"*No way*. You can do that?" I asked unbelievably, grinning all over my face.

"Architect Extraordinaire on the job, he's been waiting months for me to accept," he replied, a hint of a smile still there, "See you later, love."

"See you, dad. Assalam u alaikum."

"Wa alaikum assalam."

I shot Jayne an excited smile, "You will not believe what I just did."

"What?"

"Let's go order some Lobster first, and then I'll tell you," I said, linking arms with her and Sophie as we walked towards our lunch table, Sarah and Christy already seated and waving us down. I turned my head slightly, my eyes searching the hall until they rested on a familiar set of girls wearing hijabs, smiling at me tentatively. Grinning broadly, I beckoned them over with a wave of my hand. It was time for them to meet the other girls.

Life was just perfect, Alhamdulillah.

Epilogue

Three weeks later

"Okay, we'll have it ready for you in a few months. Please write your name and details here," the woman behind the counter smiled sweetly, passing a form to me to fill in.

I signed my name, *Asmara Anderson,* and wrote down my details as the girl beside me squealed, "Oh, this is just so great! I'm so excited! My best friend's getting married!"

"Not till another two years," I laughed, a blush already creeping onto my face, "I can't believe I'm engaged though."

We both looked down simultaneously at the diamond ring on my finger, dazzling brightly in the sunlight, and gasped, "Wow."

"He must be a very lucky man," the woman behind the counter smiled, taking in my shimmering face, and then added curiously, "You two are Muslim, and happy?"

"Extremely," the girl beside me said and held out her hand, "Jannah Collins. I've only been Muslim five days but my life already feels complete."

She shook her hand, "Well, it was a pleasure to meet you both. Thank you for visiting the Vera Wang bridal store, please come again."

"When it's my turn," Jannah winked at me, and I laughed as we stepped out of Selfridges and onto Oxford street. I smoothed down my 'abaya, an Islamic cloak intended for women to cover their bodies, with my hands as a gust of strong wind blew past and it began to drizzle lightly. We hurried towards my mum's car and I unlocked the doors, taking an extra set of keys out of my pocket, before jumping in.

"It seems like your mum's not done yet," Jannah said, shivering as I switched the heater on.

"Yeah, she must still be discussing the details with the interior designer my dad called up for her. Oh, and that reminds me, I have to make a call."

Jannah smiled at me knowingly, "Calling your husband-to-be to let him know how well the wedding plans are going?"

"Actually, no," I smirked, "I already called Jef...I mean, Yasin, in the morning. Now, if you'd excuse me, I have *another* important call to make," and then dialling a number, I put my mobile to my ear and grinned slyly as Jannah narrowed her eyes, wondering what was going on.

"Katie?"

"Hey, I was wondering if you wanted to go out for lunch tomorrow."

"You found answers, didn't you?"

2

"I found more than just answers; I found everything that I was looking for, Kitty. And I can't wait to tell you."

"Well, I can't wait to hear," she replied.

"Ringo's?"

"Done. Oh, and Katie, thank you."

"For what?"

"For realizing who you are, for being more than an average teenager, and for finding answers and calling me."

"You're welcome," I answered graciously, "but just so you know, you were a huge part of all of this, your encouragement made this happen."

As I got off the phone, I smiled inwardly and looked immediately at Jannah, relaying with my eyes just how joyful I felt. The look in her eyes told me that she was at the peak of happiness too, and I knew then that I didn't have to look too far to realize the journey it had taken for three friends to grow infinitely closer, to build a friendship that wouldn't last a few years but forever, and to discover themselves and fortunately, Islam.

The sound of the car door being yanked open and my mum plonking down on the front seat broke the moment, and I turned towards my mum as she slammed the door.

"God, it's freezing out there," she said, rubbing her hands together and turning to face us, "So how'd it go?"

"Perfectly," Jannah replied, "The dress you and Kat...Asmara

3

chose yesterday is still available and they'll have it ready in a few months. How about you?"

"The interior designer Jac...Yahya suggested is fabulous!" she grinned, "Oh, these names, they'll take some time to get used to. Well, anyways, she completely understands how I want the new salon designed. I can't believe we're actually opening up a new branch. No, wait, that's believable. I can't believe my daughter's getting married soon!"

I laughed, "Hold your horses. Two more years to go, guys."

"It's so romantic to get married at nineteen," my mum sighed happily, "I remember when your dad proposed to me at that age too. Oh, I can't wait to start planning the wedding!"

Jannah bounced up and down in glee as I rolled my eyes with a grin, "I can't believe you made me book a wedding dress from now."

"Well, I had to come up with something to match your dad's enthusiasm. Booking a beachside hotel for the wedding in Morocco two years ahead of time isn't crazy?"

I tried to fight the look of amusement on my face. Mum and Dad were constantly at each other's throats when it came to the wedding, their competitive streaks just one of the things that was going to make planning this wedding absolutely crazy.

"Oh, Jannah, I absolutely forgot to mention something to you. How would you like to be an intern at the salon?" Mum asked, "You'd get paid for your brilliant ideas."

"Oh My God! Yes!"

I chuckled and looked outside the window as the sky began to open up, the sun peeking out slowly, light flooding the city of London. How lucky was I to be a Muslim, and not just that, but to have my ultimate best friend, Jayne, and the crush I'd never realized I had, Jeff, become Muslim as well, to have my family accept me for who I am, and to have friends of a lifetime, to have my whole 'perfect' world pulled out from under me, tripping me in the process, and then for it to be replaced with an even better one as I rose up again, and all this in the space of the same year. Some might say this was nothing short of miraculous and some might say it was good fortune, but *me?* I'd say it was God's will, His blessings showered upon someone He'd chosen to become Muslim, for He was capable of anything.

I rolled down my window, as a cool gust of air caressed my face, and closed my eyes, before reciting one of my favourite du'aas under my breath.

'Radeetu billahi rabban wa bil Islami deenan wa bi Muhammadan sallallahu 'alayhi wa sallam nabiyan.'

I am pleased with Allah as my Lord, and with Islam as my Religion, and with Muhammad as the Messenger.

I'd chosen the name Asmara a week after converting to Islam, and after hours of researching names and flipping through books. When I read the meaning, I knew instantly that it was the name for me.

Beautiful butterfly. Just like a butterfly, I've gone through changes to achieve beauty, the beauty of Islam, just like a butterfly, I've grown strong wings and let myself fly unto scented gardens and open skies, and just like a butterfly, I am free.

ABOUT THE AUTHOR

At the age of 13, Safaa Baig finally discovered her answer
to one of life's most important [and truly mind-boggling]
questions, 'What do you want to be when you grow up?'
Today, some odd years later, [although her family heartily
argues that she is nowhere near grown up] she is an Islamic
novelist, writing in the hopes of touching people's hearts and
inspiring change. Her aim is to leave Islam's mark as far as she
can reach - and beyond.

On the side, she enjoys chatting people's ears off, baking
goodies to make people's tummies happy, learning exotic
languages [and of course there's a hidden agenda behind that
one too], amongst a number of other phenomenally exciting
things. She is a daydreamer at heart and a visionary in being.

'Soul of a Butterfly' is Safaa Baig's first ever published novel,
completed at the age of 17.

She has also written articles for various websites
and successfully scripted live plays for Islamic youth
organizations.

For more info and updates, book excerpts and sneak peeks,
you can follow her at her website: www.safaabaig.com

Lightning Source UK Ltd.
Milton Keynes UK
UKOW03f0602060514

231159UK00001B/1/P